For the most famous pirate of all – Grandpa Pirate!

I would also like to make special mention of Laila Altschul, winner of the 2018 Budding Illustrator Competition for her enchanting drawing of an Earie Lugger.

Contents

Chapter 1

Witches Storm

Jake the Goblin pirate was greener than usual, his stomach churning as the ship rollercoastered through the vicious waves. He'd sailed through gales before, but this one felt different.

He watched in horror as a thick grey storm cloud appeared on the horizon and came racing towards the ship, tornados of water shooting up from the sea below it. The young pirate had heard stories of Witches who could create storm clouds so fierce, that entire ships had disappeared in their wake. The hairs on the back of his neck stood to attention and his pointed Goblin ears were on full alert as the cloud rapidly advanced.

With it came a hailstorm so violent that Jake felt as though he was being bombarded with rocks.

Everything turned black and an icy chill filled the air. Jake heard a loud shriek above him, but when he looked up he could see nothing because a thick shroud of fog now surrounded the ship. Suddenly, two vivid streaks of light severed the darkness, revealing Mogdred and her two daughters, squealing like banshees as they flew towards him.

Mogdred, still furious from her defeat at the Eagalach Cup, had unleashed her rage to create the ferocious storm, the likes of which Jake had never seen before.

He dived out of the crow's nest just in time to avoid the clutches of the Night Witches. But his descent was faster than planned and he sprained his ankle as he crashed onto the wooden deck. A Witch's lightning bolt landed behind him. He tried to get up to run, but staggered and fell back down as his ankle gave way. He lay on his back, helpless, as he watched another lightning bolt come hurtling towards him. It was only inches away from his face when the ship tilted on its port side, sending everything, including Jake, across the deck.

"Are you okay?" another Goblin screamed through the rain as he pulled Jake to his feet. Jake had sailed with Sam for as long as either could remember, plundering treasure from many mysterious shores under the command of their captain, The Black Claw.

Before Jake could answer, a third Goblin pirate emerged through the torrent of rain.

"Don't just stand there holding hands!" he shouted at them. "Man the cannons..."

Tibbs was the first mate, and although considerably smaller than Jake or Sam, he was a fiery character whom neither dared cross.

"Aye, aye!" they yelled back in unison. Jake limped off below deck while Sam descended on a rope into the hull. Together they hoisted a large cannonball out of a chest and heaved it over to a rusty old cannon called Bertha. Bertha had been named after the ship's cook, who was a bit of a 'blow hard'.

"Come on you two... we've not got all day," the cannon bellowed, as it transformed from a rusty old gun into a sleek black cannon with a large round mouth in place of a front muzzle. "I can take out twenty Night Witches with one blast," Bertha boasted.

"Yes, alright Bertha, we're coming!" Jake yelled back. He was limping as he lugged the cannonball across the deck with Sam. Waves were crashing over both sides of the ship, soaking the Goblins with every inundation.

"*Hurry up!*" Bertha shouted out impatiently. "They're getting aw..." The gobby cannon was silenced mid-sentence by Jake and Sam pushing the huge cannonball into its mouth. They gave each other a cheeky wink before tilting the cannon towards the sky. Jake carefully took aim, adjusting the angle of the cannon until the target was in his sights. His target was a lumpy Night Witch with only one hand.

"Fire!" he hollered to Sam, instructing him to light the cannon fuse. Just as the words left Jake's lips the ship tilted again, throwing the cannon off target. Instead of firing up into the sky, the cannonball flew diagonally across the bow, tearing through the main sail.

Tibbs glared over at Jake from the ship's wheel, where he was desperately trying to steady the vessel. He spun the wheel frantically from left to right, trying to negotiate the craggy rocks that were piercing through the surface of the water, while simultaneously preventing the ship from capsizing under the sheer force of the waves. He glanced across the bow, then suddenly froze. He was still holding tightly to the wheel when he realised that the ship was no longer tilting. In fact, the ship wasn't moving at all! The sea was dead calm. Everything was eerily still, apart from the rain that continued thrashing down on them.

"I don't like the look of this," Sam whispered to Jake. "The water looks like tar!"

Jake wasn't paying any attention to Sam's words. He was still staring at the statuesque figure of Tibbs, wondering what could have frightened his feisty first mate so much, when suddenly, the deck beneath him started to separate.

"Jump!" Sam screamed through the rain. He launched himself towards Jake and pushed him overboard, just as an enormous spine of razor-sharp fins sliced through the deck.

Mogdred shrieked with laughter as she looked down on the ill-fated ship from her broom.

"They're in the Lurgie," her daughter Sloth cackled with delight. "The Sea Serpents have them now… there's no escape!" she squawked.

Mogdred scrutinised the scene one last time for a final gloat at the fate of the Goblin pirates, before vanishing into the night sky, Sloth and Gretch following in her wake.

Water was gushing in through the hull, dragging the vessel down into the murky sea.

Sam raced to starboard, once again dodging the Sea Serpent's razor-sharp fin, which was slicing through the middle of the ship, cutting it in two. He leapt into a small rowing boat hanging off the side and started hacking through the ropes securing it to the ship with his cutlass. He could see two huge Sea Serpents circling the sinking ship, ready to feast on the crew as they abandoned their doomed vessel.

He scoured the surface of the water but couldn't see Jake's body anywhere.

Below deck, Will, Flynn and Toby were still fast asleep in their triple bunk bed. These three Goblins could sleep through anything! They snored in unison while the ship was being torn apart by the menacing Sea Serpents.

Toby, on the bottom bunk, was dreaming about booty when he felt something wet and slimy skim the side of his foot.

"Oi, leave me alone," he mumbled dreamily, wriggling his toes.

The slimy sensation travelled along the side of his body, soaking him in the process. He shot bolt upright and opened his eyes. All he could see was two rows of Sea Serpent teeth, ready to chomp! In terror, he scrambled up to Flynn's bunk.

"Wake up!" he screamed, shaking Flynn by the shoulders.

Flynn had barely opened his eyes when he found himself being hauled up onto Will's bunk. Thankfully Will had been woken by Toby's screams and managed to pull his crewmates to safety.

The Sea Serpent had disappeared under the murky water, but there was no doubt it would soon be back.

The bottom bunk was already submerged.

"We're all going to die!" sobbed Toby as the water level reached the top bunk.

The Goblin pirates stood on their tiptoes, but within seconds the water had risen to their necks. They tilted their heads back, gasping in the last of the air left in the cabin. Suddenly, Flynn sprang up, banging his head off the ceiling.

"They're coming through the wall," he shouted, rubbing his side where he'd just been jabbed by a sharp prong.

Flynn was the smallest of the three Goblins. His crooked teeth protruded through his full lips and he had a tuft of dark curly hair that sat on the crown of his head. This was unusual – most Goblin pirates are bald!

A hole had appeared in the cabin wall and a long black prong was making its way inside. The three Goblins fumbled for their cutlasses, but the water had by now risen above their heads and was starting to fill their lungs.

Flynn was the first to be dragged through the hole, followed by Toby, whose screams were just bubbles lost in the sinister depths.

Will managed to get out his cutlass, but he was too late! The skin on his side was ripped open as he too was pulled

12

through the hole and plunged into the abyss of Sea Serpents.

A huge claw with three piercing black hooks soared towards him as he bobbed helplessly in the water. It grabbed him with one swoop and launched him into the rowing boat.

"Captain, you're alive!" Will gasped, coughing up puddles of muddy water.

Captain Bruce, also known as 'The Black Claw', was a tall slim Goblin with a large hoop-earring dangling from his left ear lobe. He wore a purple hat embossed with skull and crossbones tilted down over his right eye.

"Arrr," the captain replied. As he retracted his huge claw, it shrank down from the size of a giant octopus tentacle to that of a human hand, then his three claws merged together to form a single black hook at the end of his wrist.

When he finally stopped coughing, Will was relieved to see his two other bunk-mates sitting at the back of the boat along with Sam and Jake, who was lying at their feet, unconscious. All of them were bruised and bleeding, and blood was dripping from Will's wound onto the deck.

"Here, wrap this around your waist," first mate Tibbs instructed Will, handing him a piece of cloth. "Sea Serpents can smell blood a mile away," he continued in a low tone, scanning the waves.

"That's everyone accounted for, captain," whispered Sam, keeping a watchful eye on the water.

"And the chest?" the captain asked anxiously.

"It's on board." Sam nodded towards a wooden chest at the stern of the boat.

The captain let out a small sigh of relief. "Dead slow ahead," he whispered.

With Tibbs and Sam standing at either side of the boat keeping lookout, Flynn and Toby began rowing through the Lurgie. Progress was painfully slow and they had hardly made any distance when Tibbs urgently signalled them to stop rowing.

"Shh, don't move a muscle," he said, placing his index finger onto his lips.

The Goblin pirates watched motionless as a massive fin emerged from the water. The Sea Serpent circled the boat, deliberating where to strike, when:

"Come and get me, you scurvy dog!" bellowed Bertha. The cannon was floating on the surface of the water surrounded by pieces of shipwreck.

Momentarily distracted, the Sea Serpent disappeared under the water, only to emerge seconds later. Jaws wide open, it charged forward, intending to swallow Bertha whole. Just as it closed its jaws Bertha gave them a cheeky wink and mouthed "Fire!"

"*Row...* row like the wind!" Tibbs yelled. The entire crew grabbed hold of the oars and pulled.

The captain looked back over his shoulder just in time to see the Sea Serpent's head explode.

"Bertha's gone down with the ship," he muttered mournfully as they rowed out of the Lurgie.

"It's what she would've wanted, captain," Tibbs reassured him.

Chapter 2

Smidge

Thumble Tumble was waiting patiently by the open window, wondering what time Skye would appear. Skye was one of the Water Fairies who lived in the magical waterfalls found at the far end of the Light and Dark forest. These tiny fairies have a very special job on the Isle of Arran. On each full moon they sprinkle every child on the island with fairy dust that protects them from Night Witches until the next full moon.

Skye was Thumble Tumble's fairy. Normally, these transparent little fairies go about their business completely undetected, invisible to the children they protect. However, Thumble Tumble was no ordinary child and she could see and hear Skye perfectly.

Skye's timing had always been a little erratic. She'd leave the waterfall just before midnight with all the other fairies, but then get distracted by something and end up drifting off to investigate. This resulted in her arriving at Thumble Tumble's bedroom window any time between midnight and 2 a.m.

It had already gone past two and there was still no sign of Skye.

"What on earth could be taking her so long?" Thumble Tumble mumbled anxiously to Flopsy, her pink fluffy cat, who was purring quietly on her lap.

"That's it, I'm going to find her!" Thumble Tumble announced. The unexpected outburst gave Flopsy such a fright that she dug her claws into Thumble Tumble's thigh.

"Ouch!" Thumble Tumble leapt into the air, dropping poor Flopsy head-first onto the floor. Just then Skye arrived at the window. "Are you okay?" she gasped.

"I'm fine," replied Thumble Tumble, rubbing her thighs. "It's you we've been worried about. Where have you been?"

Skye flew into the bedroom and began chattering excitedly. "I left the waterfall just before midnight and headed along the path through the forest. Somehow, I managed to get separated from the other fairies… I think it may have been when I went off to look at some unusual looking beetles," she added vaguely. "Anyway, when I reached the end of the forest, I came across a large wooden chest with the head of a beautiful young woman carved into its lid. The chest was sitting on the shore beside an upturned rowing boat. I was about to peek inside the chest when two horrible Tree Trolls appeared, so I hid under the boat. They were bragging about how they had captured 'The Black Claw' and how Mogdred was sure to reward them for bringing her his treasure chest. They picked up the chest by its handles and headed into the forest with it."

When she'd finished talking, Skye twirled in the air and took a little bow.

"I've never heard of The Black Claw," Thumble Tumble said curiously, "but I know who the Tree Trolls are – Ugg and Ogg, Mogdred's moronic henchmen. I think we'd better investigate what they're up to before they get a chance to contact Mogdred," she said, pulling her broom out from under her bed.

Thumble Tumble was already dressed and she had her red cloak packed away in the little basket attached to her broom. "Always prepared," she grinned, then she jumped onto her broom and flew out of the open window with Skye close on her heels.

Shaking her head in despair, Flopsy watched Thumble Tumble and Skye fly off. Then she curled up in a ball and fell asleep.

They followed the shoreline, their route illuminated by the moonlight. "Down there," said Skye, pointing to the upturned boat. They flew down and landed on the shore beside the boat. The Tree Trolls had left a trail in the sand where they'd dragged the chest.

Thumble Tumble tucked her broom under the boat then took out her wand. "Irradiate!" she uttered, and a small white light appeared at the tip of her wand. "This way," she said, then started following the trail into the Light and Dark Forest.

Skye perched on Thumble Tumble's shoulder as they made their way through the thick foliage. Inside the forest the canopy of treetops blocked out the moonlight and it was eerily dark. The dense air was filled with a musky aroma from the carpet of leaves on the forest floor. The damp, mushy leaves squelched as Thumble Tumble walked over them, her foot slurping into the mud with each step.

Every time a twig skimmed her face, Thumble Tumble leapt in the air – the sensation felt the same as a Night Witches' talons stroking her cheeks.

"Which way do we go?" Skye asked nervously. Skye had never ventured off the main path through the forest before, and for good reason. The Light and Dark Forest had been given its name because although the central path was brightly lit, as soon anyone stepped off it, they were swamped in a cloak of darkness. If you left that path, it would prove almost impossible to find it again!

"I'm pretty sure it's this way," Thumble Tumble said confidently, pointing her wand in the direction of a gaping hole in the foliage where the Tree Trolls had crashed through, leaving a trail of destruction behind them.

Thumble Tumble and Skye followed the newly formed path of broken branches and twigs, all the while feeling that someone was watching them. Thumble Tumble was sure she caught sight of a pair of eyes peering through the foliage, but when she looked back, they disappeared! She spun round and called out "Revelio!" A blast of light flew out from her wand and illuminated the figure now standing right behind them. It was a brightly coloured Tweezel Berry bush, with yellow leaves and purple berries dangling off its branches.

"What are you doing here?" Thumble Tumble gasped.

The Tweezel Berry bush paused for a moment before its branches parted, revealing a small bird sitting in its centre.

The bird resembled a robin, but instead of having a red breast, its tummy was covered in vibrant orange feathers and it had a spiky mohawk on its head to match.

"I didn't mean to scare you," the little bird tweeted.

"My name's Smidge. I'm a hatchling worker."

"A hatchling worker?" Skye quizzed, frowning.

"I carry eggs to the great hatchling tree so the chicks can hatch safely," the little bird replied. "I was carrying an egg to the hatchling tree last night when I decided to have a quick twenty winks. I placed the egg onto the lid of an old wooden chest that was lying on the beach and closed my eyes for literally two minutes. When I woke up, the chest was gone, along with my egg. You two then appeared and I overheard you chatting about finding the chest, so I decided to follow you to see if you could lead me to my missing egg."

"Oh, my goodness," gasped Skye. "Your poor egg!"

Smidge's eyes filled with tears and a massive lump appeared in his throat. His beak opened, but he was too choked to tweet.

"Don't worry," said Thumble Tumble reassuringly. "We'll help you find your egg."

A huge smile spread across Smidge's face and his tears quickly changed to tears of joy.

He flapped his wings to fly out of the Tweezel Berry bush, but the bush suddenly threw its branches back around him.

"Let me go!" Smidge snapped.

Thumble Tumble and Skye were both surprised at the little bird's angry tone.

Spotting the concerned look they exchanged, Smidge continued in a much softer tone. "You can let me go now," he whispered gently. "I'll be okay with Thumble Tumble."

The bush reluctantly spread open its branches and Smidge flew over to Thumble Tumble, perching on the opposite shoulder from Skye. The Tweezel Berry bush floated a few inches off the ground and began hovering backwards in the direction of the shore.

"Goodbye," said Thumble Tumble, waving.

She then resumed her journey along the path of destruction created by the Tree Trolls with Skye as her lookout. Smidge, however, kept staring back at the Tweezel Berry bush, glaring at it until it had completely disappeared into the forest. He then spun round on Thumble Tumble's shoulder, and as he did, his dark expression changed into a sweet smile.

Chapter 3

The Sleeping Death

The journey into the forest was taking a lot longer than Thumble Tumble anticipated. The sun began to rise, allowing small shards of light to penetrate the thick tree canopy.

"How much further do you think we have to go?" groaned Skye. "I'm tired and hungry," she continued with a big yawn.

Skye lay on Thumble Tumble's shoulder, barely able to keep her eyes open. Sun up was bedtime for Water Fairies, as they spent every night flying around sprinkling fairy dust on sleeping children. Because of this nocturnal behaviour they were sometimes referred to as 'Vampire Fairies' – not a very appropriate nickname in the human world, where vampires are bloodsucking monsters. Thankfully, the nickname has never crossed over from the magical realm to the human world.

"I hope it's not too much longer," Thumble Tumble replied through a huge yawn of her own. "Perhaps we should rest for a while?"

"You don't need a rest," Smidge chirped into the conversation. "I'm sure it can't be much further." He flew up off Thumble Tumble's shoulder. "There, that should help," he announced.

To Thumble Tumble's surprise, it really did. The tiny bird was all of ten centimetres tall, but when it flew off her shoulder it felt as though a huge boulder had just been lifted.

"You're pretty heavy for such a wee bird," exclaimed Thumble Tumble.

"Looks can be deceiving," grinned Smidge. He flew ahead, leading them further into the forest.

Skye was fast asleep, so Thumble Tumble gently lifted her off her shoulder and popped her into the pocket on the front of her dress.

After she'd been walking for another hour, Thumble Tumble's stomach started to complain. At first there was a gurgle every few minutes, then a rumbling that got louder and louder.

"I think we need to get you something to eat," chirped Smidge.

"Me too," replied Thumble Tumble. "But Smidge, that last growl wasn't me!"

She stood completely still and listened.

Smidge flew up to the top branch of a tree to try to see where the growling noise was coming from.

"It's over there," he tweeted, pointing his left wing.

"That's weird," replied Thumble Tumble. "I was sure it was coming from the other direction."

Thumble Tumble took a step in the direction Smidge was pointing and promptly fell into a ditch. The ditch had been covered over with twigs so she couldn't see it, and it was so deep that even the tip of her hat wasn't visible.

Within seconds two familiar faces were peering down at her. Both had huge, bulbous heads with sunken, black, oval eyes and round, craggy mouths. The creatures looked almost identical, with their scrawny bodies covered head to toe in bark. The only difference was that one of them had a stump in place of his left foot.

"What do we have here?" Ugg grinned, tapping the side of the ditch with his stump.

"It's Thumble Tumble," replied Ogg nodding, feeling very pleased with his answer.

Thumble Tumble had crossed paths with Ugg and Ogg before. The dim-witted Tree Trolls were Mogdred's henchmen.

"I know it's Thumble Tumble," Ugg screamed into his twin's face. "It was a retractable question!"

"I think you mean rhetorical question," Thumble Tumble shouted up from the ditch.

"It's got nothing to do with history, *or you!*" Ugg snarled back, prodding her hat with his stump. "Hand over your wand," he continued, growling at her.

Thumble Tumble slowly took her wand out from her pocket. There was a rebellious glint in her eye. She was thinking about the words to her vapourising spell inside her head as she gradually pointed the wand upwards.

"I wouldn't do that," smirked Ugg and he thrust his branch-like hand over the ditch. In it was clenched Smidge's tiny body. Ugg grinned maliciously and began shaking Smidge's body like a baby's rattle.

With his index finger wrapped tightly around the little bird's throat, he started swinging its body from side to side. Smidge began to turn blue. His beak was snapping

frantically and he tried to draw breath, but no air could squeeze past the noose around his neck.

"Let him go – you're killing him!" screamed Thumble Tumble as she threw her wand up out of the ditch.

Ugg instantly released his grip, then looked sheepishly over at his twin brother and gently placed Smidge on the ground.

"Get the net," instructed Ogg. The pair of them pulled a huge net over the ditch and fastened it to the ground with wooden pegs.

When the colour finally returned to Smidge's cheeks, he glared at Ugg, then tweeted arrogantly, "Huh, that net won't hold Thumble Tumble!"

"That's right," Ogg answered for his brother. "But this

will!" He held up a glass vial filled with a thick yellow liquid, pulled out the cork and placed the open container beside the net.

"Be careful," Ugg shouted, pushing his brother's hand away from the liquid oozing out of the container. "If a single drop of that Sleeping Death Potion touches you, you'll fall into a deep sleep from which you'll never wake up!"

The Tree Trolls both took a giant step backwards and watched as the potion leaked out, forming a puddle on the ground. After a few seconds, the body of a snake emerged from the centre of the puddle, hissing and lunging towards the Trolls before it turned and coiled itself around the spaces in the net.

Thumble Tumble crouched down as much as she could, pulling off her hat just in time to avoid it being covered by the potion.

"I think *that* will hold her until Mogdred gets here," Ogg sniggered at Smidge.

He carefully picked up the little bird. "You're coming with us," he said, and they headed deeper into the forest.

Chapter 4

Fairy Genius

The dim light that had been covering the ditch disappeared as night fell, leaving Thumble Tumble in complete darkness. She was crouched low to the ground, shivering from the cold night air. She had all but forgotten the strange wooden chest on the beach as she contemplated the horrors of what Mogdred might do to her when she arrived, which wouldn't be long now that night had fallen.

As she stared into the darkness, she could feel her stomach begin to squirm. *That's all I need*, she thought. *As well as being trapped in this hole surrounded by poison, I'm beginning to starve!*

But strangely, she didn't feel hungry. She rubbed her stomach with her hand to investigate the cause of the squirming sensation. "Oi... be careful!" a small voice echoed through the darkness.

"Is that you, Skye?" gasped Thumble Tumble excitedly, fumbling in the dark to find her small companion.

"Who else were you expecting to pop out of your pocket?" Skye replied cheerily. "And why are we in a ditch?" she continued, not quite as chirpily, as she began to take in her surroundings.

"It was those horrible Tree Trolls. They trapped me in this ditch so that Mogdred can get me!"

A bright shimmer began to emanate from Skye's body, making her look like a little glow-worm. The light grew so strong that she lit up the ditch.

"Why don't you just cast a spell to get us out of here? Or better still, just climb out?" Skye quizzed, hovering up towards the net covering the ditch.

"Don't touch that!" screamed Thumble Tumble, and grabbed Skye's entire body in her hand. Just as she pulled Skye away, a long, yellow, forked tongue darted out from the net.

"They covered the net with a Sleeping Death Potion," exclaimed Thumble Tumble, as she gently placed Skye on the ground.

"Can't you just blast through it with your wand?" asked Skye.

"I don't have my wand," Thumble Tumble replied wearily. "I had to give it to the Trolls to stop them from killing Smidge. They were going to strangle him!"

"Oh well, looks like we're *doomed*," said Skye smirking.

"It's no laughing matter," Thumble Tumble retorted. "If Mogdred gets her hands on us... I dread to think what she'll do!"

"Well then we'd better not let her get her hands on us then!" Skye chipped back. She stood up, put her hands above her head with her fingers stretched out and flew straight up through one of the holes in the net. Six poison snake-heads lunged after her, but they were too slow, and

27

by the time Thumble Tumble realised what was happening, Skye was already whizzing about above the ditch.

"You're crazy!" she shouted up at her fairy guardian.

"A little," Skye agreed. She flew over to one of the wooden pegs holding the net in place and yanked it out of the ground with one heave.

"Please be careful," Thumble Tumble pleaded as she watched anxiously through the net. The tiny Water Fairy's translucent body was darting from peg to peg, with the Sleeping Death snake potion close on her heels.

When she had pulled out the final peg, Skye picked up a branch and slid it under one of the corners of the net.

But as soon as the tip of the branch touched the net, the potion slithered along it, hissing and lunging towards Skye. She tried to pick up a longer branch, but it was too heavy.

"I've got an idea," she announced, then she dashed into the trees.

A moment later she reappeared with a handful of dried leaves. She flew into the air and began dropping the leaves one at a time onto the ground to form a chain. As each leaf landed, the poison slithered along the chain towards Skye. Eventually it had slithered so far along the chain of leaves that there was no poison left on the net. Skye quickly flew back to the start of the chain and blew with all her might. The leaves scattered leaving a big gap between the net and chain. Droplets of Sleeping Death Potion screeched up from the scattered leaves, but they were too small to get back onto the net.

Thumble Tumble scrambled up the inside of the ditch and pushed off the net, before clambering out to freedom.

"You're a genius, Skye!"

Skye winked back. "There is a saying in the fairy world that states: '*The craziest fairies are the most ingenious*'. And another that says: '*When you've just escaped the Sleeping Death you should RUN!*'"

Thumble Tumble was in total agreement. She jumped to her feet and started sprinting in the direction the Tree Trolls had gone, with Skye's glowing body just in front of her to light the way.

When they were sure they were out of the clutches of the Sleeping Death Potion, they gradually slowed down.

"We need to get you out of here," exclaimed Skye. "Those Tree Trolls will definitely have contacted Mogdred by now, and if she finds you, she'll kill you! She'll do anything to get her hands on your powers. And the only way to take the Protector's power is if the Protector is dead. And speaking of death, I almost forgot your fairy dust!" She clapped her hands and a twinkling silver powder appeared, floating in mid-air. Skye swept her hand through the powder, sprinkling it over Thumble Tumble's body.

"There you go," Skye said in a tone of satisfaction. "Now Mogdred can't touch you. Well, not until the next full moon."

Thumble Tumble could smell a nasty odour wafting up from the dust that had settled on her dress.

"That's strange," she said.

"What is?" asked Skye.

"There isn't usually a horrible smell from fairy dust."

"That's not fairy dust," said Skye, scrunching her nose as the foul smell reached her nostrils.

Thumble Tumble looked down at her feet to find she was standing beside a huge pile of Troll droppings.

"Arghhh!" she screamed as she leapt back from the offensive dung.

"Be quiet," whispered Skye. "The Trolls must be close – those droppings look fresh!" she continued, almost gagging.

Skye perched herself back on Thumble Tumble's shoulder and they continued to creep through the foliage. It wasn't long before they reached a clearing.

"That's them," Thumble Tumble whispered, pointing towards a makeshift campsite where a number of Goblins, wearing eye patches, hoop earings and hats embossed with skull and cross bones, were sitting bound and gagged, on the ground.

The Trolls were prodding and poking the captured Goblin pirates, demanding that the captain reveal himself. To the left of the captors there was a huge wooden chest with a carving of a beautiful young woman etched into its lid.

"That's the chest from the beach," Skye said in a hushed tone.

"But where's Smidge and his egg?" asked Thumble Tumble.

As they edged forward, they were once again overwhelmed by the disgusting odour of Troll poo.

"You must have stood in it!" exclaimed Skye, looking down at Thumble Tumble's shoes in disgust.

She turned to fly away from the horrible smell and found herself face-to-face with its source. It wasn't another giant pile of Troll dropping – it was Mogdred herself, grinning menacingly with her foul breath seeping through the spaces between her pointy black teeth.

Mogdred thrust her hand towards Thumble Tumble and

wrapped her long bony fingers around her neck. "What were you saying?" she asked as she began to squeeze. "That I'd need to prise the ring off of your dead body to take the Protector's Powers?" She howled with laughter as she tightened her grip around Thumble Tumble's throat.

Moments before she throttled Thumble Tumble, Mogdred let out an ear-piercing shriek. She pulled her hand from Thumble Tumble's throat and looked down to see the skin on her palm scorched with pieces of burned flesh poking through her skin.

"Fairy dust!" she yelped.

"Oh well, it won't last forever, just until the next full moon!" She flicked her damaged hand in the air and a long vine came darting out of the foliage. It wrapped itself around Thumble Tumble like a python, coiling upwards from her feet to the tip of her head, finally rendering her unconscious as it wrapped around her nose and mouth.

"What have you done?" squealed Skye.

"Unfortunately, I've just put her to sleep. *Your* fairy dust is keeping her alive... for now!" Mogdred growled at Skye.

Skye spun round to make a quick escape.

"Not so fast, my pretty!" cackled Mogdred. She clicked her fingers and a huge green bug appeared from nowhere and came buzzing towards Skye with its jaws wide open.

Skye quickly resumed her position.

"No snacks for now," said Mogdred, calling off the green beastie.

She mumbled a spell that lifted Thumble Tumble's entangled body a few inches off the ground. Then she made her way into the campsite with Thumble Tumble's bound body hovering behind her.

Chapter 5

The Black Claw

When Mogdred arrived at the campsite she found one of the Goblins dangling upside down from a tree and Ugg was poking him in the stomach with his long twig-like finger, screaming, "Tell me where the key is!" Ugg was also using a variety of scary facial contortions to frighten the Goblin into submission. This, of course, was a complete waste of time, as he was shouting at the Goblin's feet.

"What are you doing, you imbecile?" screeched Mogdred, pushing the Troll onto the ground.

"I'm interrogating the captain to find out where the key to the chest is," Ugg replied sheepishly.

"Then why do you have the first mate hanging by his toes?" Mogdred spluttered into his face.

The Night Witch floated over to the chest and pointed a long craggy finger at the lock. "Liberationous!"

The lock on the chest began vibrating. Mogdred smiled wickedly. But her smile changed to a snarl when the vibrating suddenly stopped, with the chest still firmly locked.

Mogdred placed the palm of her hand onto the lid of the chest and bellowed at the top of her voice, "I command you by all the powers of evil to liberate this chest."

The lock immediately started shaking violently, thrashing itself against the lid. Mogdred looked back over towards the Goblins with a sneering, smug look of satisfaction. But the sneer was wiped off her face when the lock once again resumed its original position, with the chest still intact. Furious, she rounded on the crew of Goblin pirates, glaring directly at the captain.

"The infamous Black Claw," she growled. The captain found himself being pulled to his feet by an invisible force. It dragged him up off the ground and thrust his body towards Mogdred until he was so close, the tip of his nose touched hers, his rigid body tightly bound by her evil spell, leaving him absolutely helpless.

Despite his predicament, the captain seemed unfazed. In fact, there appeared to be a smirk on his face.

"You won't be smiling for long," Mogdred spat at him. She slid her tongue across his cheek then smacked her lips. "Mmm, Goblin cheek, my favourite dessert!"

"I've always wondered what Witch dessert tastes like," the captain replied, still smiling. "Now I know… it tastes like me!" he laughed heartily.

"No, no, no!" Mogdred said, shaking her head. "Them!" She pointed towards the Goblin crew.

"One by one you'll watch them be cooked and eaten, and *then* we'll eat you!" She turned to the crew, scrutinising each of them in turn.

"Who shall be first?" she cackled, reaching out to squeeze her hand tightly around Will's bony arm. Beads of sweat started pouring from his forehead.

"Too thin," she announced. Will breathed a huge sigh of relief. "We'll have to fatten you up first," she added, with an obnoxious laugh.

Tibbs was the next Goblin to attract her malevolent attention. He lay on the ground, writhing in agony – his toenails had been pulled out because he had been dangling upside down for so long.

"Not you either," she said kicking Tibbs out of her way. "You're in too much pain already. We'll wait until you're feeling better so we can appreciate torturing you before we eat you."

Tibbs did not respond to her jibes.

Mogdred's eyes moved along the line of Goblins and set on Jake. Mogdred noticed the bandages around his crumpled leg and she looked him up and down dismissively, before moving on to Sam. She noticed the relief in Sam's eyes that Jake was no longer being considered and an evil grin spread across her face. "You'll do!" she hollered, clenching Jake's face in her hands.

Ugg and Ogg grabbed Jake under his arms and dragged him towards the large fire that was blazing in the centre of the campsite.

Sam struggled to free himself from his bindings. "Leave him alone," he yelled.Ugg and Ogg continued dragging Jake's limp body towards the fire.

"I can get you the key," Sam shouted anxiously.

"Hold on!" Mogdred commanded the Trolls.

"Okay, then give it to me," she demanded, her hand outstretched.

Sam could see maggots crawling down from under Mogdred's sleeve onto her hand.

"First let him go," Sam shouted defiantly.

"Drop him," Mogdred barked at Ugg and Ogg.

The Trolls reluctantly let go of Jake's arms and he crashed face-first onto the ground.

"Not fair," muttered Ugg, looking over at his brother with a defiant glint in his eye. Ogg shook his head. He knew that if they didn't obey Mogdred, they would be next on the fire.

"We've let him go, now give me the key," Mogdred demanded. Her outstretched hand was now completely covered in maggots.

"I need to get it before I can give it to you," Sam replied.

Morgdred lunged forward gripping Sam by the throat. "Don't play games with me," she shrieked.

"I'm not," he gasped. "It's Medusa's chest."

Mogdred threw Sam to the ground then floated over to the chest. "Rise my Queen," she said, staring at the chest. Nothing happened.

She swung back towards Sam in a fit of fury, then suddenly her expression changed and she once again floated over to the chest, whispering eerily.

"Queen of darkness,

Heart of stone,

Reveal your image,

For blood and bone."

She picked a handful of Tibbs' bloody toenails off the ground and dropped them onto the lid of the chest.

The image of the woman's face began to move. Her long hair floated up off the chest and changed from a flat two-dimensional image into a three-dimensional mop of golden hair blowing in the breeze.

Then the full head floated up off the top of the chest,

35

changing from 2D to 3D as it did so. The beautiful woman opened her mouth as if to speak, but instead of words coming out, a loud hideous shriek echoed through the campsite like a siren. The woman's eyes sunk into her head turning into two black holes and her golden locks transformed into a mass of hissing snakes.

"My Queen," Mogdred gushed as she bowed before the image.

"Who has called me from my slumber?" hissed Medusa.

"Mogdred, Supreme Night Witch and loyal servant," Mogdred grovelled.

"Why have you woken me?"

"To free you, my Queen," Mogdred said in an obsequious tone.

"To free me you must find the key. And for this I will reward you greatly."

"Where is the key, my Queen?"

"The key lies at Worlds End," boomed Medusa, then she disappeared, leaving the etched image of a young woman on the lid of the chest once again.

Chapter 6

A Crew is Formed

Hours passed as Mogdred conjured dozens of magical maps of the world trying to find 'World's End'. She looked in Poseidon's charts of the seas, Loki's plans plotting the underworld and even took Admiral Horatio Nelson's atlas from the human world to find the whereabouts of World's End.

She painstakingly examined every diagram and drawing, looking for the slightest clue as to where the end of the world might be, but there was no trace of it. Furious, she rounded on Sam. "Do you know where it is?" she seethed.

Sam's head dropped. "No," he muttered.

"Then you're of no use to me!" Mogdred thrust her index finger towards Sam's chest.

"I know where it is!" Skye shouted as loudly as she could, flying into Mogdred's line of fire. "Well... I mean, I know someone... who knows where it is!" she stuttered nervously. "McCools, he'll know where World's End is."

"Of course!" Mogdred replied nodding. "But he's

unlikely to toddle off to the end of the world for me!" she screeched, covering poor Skye in a spray of saliva.

"But he will for her," Skye replied, pointing at Thumble Tumble, who was still fast asleep, encapsulated in her floating trap.

Mogdred had almost forgotten about Thumble Tumble, she'd been so engrossed with trying to find World's End.

"Perhaps," Mogdred mumbled under her breath. She waved her hand, releasing Thumble Tumble from her spell.

Thumble Tumble's body dropped to the ground, slamming hard onto the solid forest floor. It took her a few seconds before she clambered to her feet.

"I have a little job for you," Mogdred said. "I need you to ask that three-legged abomination, McCools, how to find Worlds End."

"McCools will never help you," gasped Thumble Tumble, still trying to re-fill her lungs with air.

"I hope *you* can persuade him," Mogdred replied raising her eyebrows. "For her sake," she nodded towards Skye, who was now in the grip of the big green bug. The bug had six legs, two of which were clutching Skye's tiny arms. It had bulging eyes and two pincers that continuously opened and snapped shut.

"You stay away from her," screamed Thumble Tumble.

The bugs eyes momentarily bulged in the direction of Thumble Tumble before refocusing back on its prey – Skye!

Thumble Tumble's eyes became red and swollen.

"Oh, don't be such a wuss," said Mogdred in a tone of disdain. "He won't eat her until I tell him he can. If you can convince your friend McCools to take you to the end of the world and bring me back the key to Medusa's chest, I will let her go," she lied.

Thumble Tumble nodded despondently.

"What was that – I couldn't quite hear you," said Mogdred, clasping her hand to her ear.

"Yes," snapped Thumble Tumble. "I'll bring you your key!"

"Good," replied Mogdred. "Now, if you're going to sail to the end of the world, you're going to need someone who can actually sail."

She spun round towards the Goblin pirates. "Any volunteers?" she shrieked. There was no response.

"Perhaps a little motivation may help," she cackled and she began twisting her index finger in the air.

Suddenly Jake flew up into the air. His body was like a piece of tissue being thrashed around in the wind, as Mogdred's spell twisted around his tired limbs.

"Let him go!" cried Sam. He ran towards Jake's flying torso, but Ugg popped out his stump and Sam fell face-first on the ground.

"My goodness," laughed Mogdred. "We seem to have a bit of a theme going on. Everyone wants me to let someone else go. Pay attention. I will release the fairy and the crew, but only when you bring me the key to Medusa's chest."

"Even if this fellow McCool's does have a map to the end of the world, how on earth do you expect us to navigate there?" asked Sam.

"Birds are good at navigating, aren't they?" she replied.

"I suppose so," Sam shrugged.

"Get me the bird," Mogdred hollered towards Ugg.

Ugg stared at her blankly.

"The little bird with the *orange feathers,*" she emphasised.

"Oh, *that* bird," said Ugg, sounding unsure.

"YES!" screamed Mogdred.

Ugg disappeared into the trees. Fifteen minutes passed before he returned, holding a very angry looking Smidge in his twiggy clutches.

"Voilà!" Mogdred gestured towards Smidge, who glared back at her.

"We have a navigator, a sailor and a Witch!" she smiled wickedly. "All you need now is a three-legged map-bearer and you'll have the perfect crew for your journey to the end of the world. If you complete your voyage and bring me back the key, your friends will be released. But, if you fail me, it will be scrambled egg and fairy cake for breakfast, with a generous helping of Goblin stew on the side."

Ugg and Ogg began salivating at the thought of such a feast.

Fists clenched, Thumble Tumble lunged towards Mogdred, but Mogdred simply flicked her wrist and the young Witch was sent hurtling through the air. She smashed into Ogg's trunk-like torso and landed in a heap at his feet.

"I'm not quite sure if you're brave, or just stupid," smirked Mogdred, glancing down at Thumble Tumble's crumpled body.

"Speaking of stupid, you seem to have forgotten one vital component," Sam interjected. His green face had almost turned brown (the colour a Goblin turns when they're angry).

"A ship!" he announced.

"Your ship will be waiting at the Ferry Port at midnight. Don't be late!"

With those words, Mogdred waved her hand in a sweeping motion, blasting all three crew members with a transporting spell.

Thumble Tumble bent over with pain as the spell ripped through her insides like a hot poker. Then it was gone, as quickly as it had come.

Thumble Tumble stood up to find herself outside a bright red door with a large silver knocker. She was holding her wand.

Sam came hurtling out of the sky and landed in the snow right beside her, then Smidge fluttered down behind him.

Chapter 7

Slumbering Giants

Initially McCools greeted Thumble Tumble in his usual grumpy manner, then he thrust his arms around her and almost crushed her with an enormous hug.

He was more reserved with her two companions, looking them up and down for a few moments before finally inviting them in.

Indoors, he prepared a large pot of thistle tea and stacked a plate with his favourite dandelion cookies, one of which he crushed into tiny crumbs which he put in a small bowl for Smidge.

Everyone made themselves comfortable in front of the open fire in the lounge, McCools in the middle, Sam on his left and Thumble Tumble on his right. Smidge perched on her shoulder, balancing his bowl of crumbs on the rim of her hat.

Thumble Tumble filled their host in on the previous evening's events, starting from when Skye arrived on her window sill, through to being transported to his front door.

"So let me get this straight," he said. "Mogdred has

captured your captain and the entire Goblin pirate crew," he nodded to Sam. "Your egg," he tilted his head towards Smidge. "And, your Water Fairy guardian," he finished, looking sympathetically into Thumble Tumble's swollen red eyes.

"And if we don't bring her the key to Medusa's chest, she'll eat all of them!" Thumble Tumble replied gloomily.

"Well, the first thing we're going to need is the map that leads us to World's End," said McCools.

"Isn't it upstairs in your library?" quizzed Thumble Tumble.

"I'm afraid not," McCools replied, shaking his head.

"I did have the map at one time, but I traded it."

"You traded it!" squawked Smidge, almost choking on his biscuit crumbs.

"So, you speak," said McCools inquisitively. This was the first time he had heard Smidge's voice since his visitors arrived.

Thumble Tumble was staring at him anxiously.

"Don't worry, I know who has it," McCools reassured her, patting her on the shoulder. "Or perhaps we should worry," he continued, looking more sombre.

"It was a few years ago," he said launching into his story.

"I was foraging for dandelions around the shores of Dohmain Loch when I spotted a rare triple-winged butterfly. I followed it up into the hills, so mesmerised by its beauty that I didn't realise where I was going.

"I was hopping through the grass watching it through my magnifying glass as it fluttered gracefully from flower to flower, the sun glistening on its magnificent turquoise wings. Then, without warning a giant foot came crashing

44

down from nowhere. It flattened twenty flowers in one go, crushing my beautiful butterfly in the process.

"I was so mad that instead of standing perfectly still (which is what I should have done), I screamed at the creature from the top of my lungs. I called him a big-footed oaf.

"Rhino, a rather nasty Spike Backed Giant, did not like being called…"

"An oaf?" Thumble Tumble butted in.

"No… big-footed!" answered McCools with raised eyebrows.

He continued his tale.

"The giant picked me up by my middle foot and had me dangling above his lips. That's when I suggested a trade. I had the map tucked into the fold in my scarf. I took it out and told him it showed the location of every three-legged haggis in the world. Not actually a lie, as I am the only three-legged haggis and I was holding it! I told him if he released me I'd give him the map."

"Why didn't he just take the map off of you and then eat you anyway?" asked Sam.

"Thankfully Spike Backed Giants aren't very bright," McCools smiled back. "But they are extremely brutal, so it won't be easy getting the map back."

"We don't have much time," Thumble Tumble interjected. "Mogdred told us to be at the Ferry Port by midnight."

"We'd better get going then," replied McCools. "Just let me get a book for the trip."

"Do you *really* need to take a book?" Thumble Tumble frowned with frustration.

"It's a boat book," McCools replied chirpily.

"Extremely useful when going on a journey involving a boat." He headed upstairs, returning just a few moments later.

"There, that didn't take long. Now all we need to do is steal a magical map from a giant."

McCools grabbed a tatty old Witch's broom from his broom cupboard. "You'll need this," he said, thrusting it into Thumble Tumble's hands. "I've got just enough broom powder to get us to the Giant Hills," he said, holding up a small brown pouch filled with sparkly silver powder.

Outside, Sam, Thumble Tumble and McCools all

squeezed onto the broomstick then McCools poured the contents of the pouch over the handle.

Thumble Tumble waved her wand and called out, "Giant Hills!"

The broom instantly lifted its passengers off the ground and flew off in the direction of the Giant Hills, with Smidge flying closely behind them.

It was already past ten o'clock in the evening when they arrived at the top of the Giant Hills.

"We've not got long," said Thumble Tumble, landing the broom gently on the ground.

"Then there's no time to waste," said McCools. "Giants go to bed around eight o'clock, so Rhino should be asleep by now." He turned to Sam. "You must be good at stealing things," he said. "No offence, but you are a pirate."

Sam winked, "Aye, aye, that I am."

"Good show," said McCools. "Rhino keeps the map under his feet when he sleeps. All you need to do is swap the map for something the same size, like a log or some bark."

Sam nodded in acknowledgement.

"You keep look-out," McCools said, directing Smidge to the top of an old oak tree.

"And you'll need to be ready with your wand in case he wakes up," he said to Thumble Tumble.

Sam began creeping through the undergrowth in the direction of the loud snoring that was making the air tremble. Not even a twig creaked underfoot as he moved undetected through the long grass. When he reached where Rhino was lying asleep on the ground, Sam scanned his surroundings looking for an object that was about the same size as the map. He could see the map, rolled up like a scroll, acting as a foot rest for the giant. The best replacement would be a log, he thought. Sam was in luck. Just a few inches from Rhino's feet was the perfect size of log. He slowly rolled the log towards Rhino's feet being careful not to disturb any dried leaves or sleeping bugs. When the log was just touching the tip of Rhino's toes, Sam put his left arm under the giant's feet, taking their weight before gingerly taking hold of the map with his right hand. Just as he started to remove the map, Rhino let out a snort and Sam froze on the spot. It took all of his strength to maintain his position and hold up the giant's feet.

Rhino's nose twitched a few times, then he resumed snoring.

Sam's left bicep burning under the strain, he slowly pulled out the map with his right hand and rolled the log in its place. When he was sure the log was in the correct position, he gently slipped his arm out from under Rhino's feet.

Grinning like a Cheshire Cat, Sam picked up the map and tiptoed back towards McCools and Thumble Tumble.

Thumble Tumble returned his smile before heading back to the broom. As she turned, she stepped on a tiny leaf. There was the slightest crinkling noise, no louder than a flee hopping.

Thumble Tumble's heart started racing. She glanced over her shoulder and let out a gentle sigh, relieved to see Rhino still lying on the ground snoring.

"Phew that was close," she whispered.

"Yes," replied a growling voice from behind them. "You nearly woke up Rhino! But as he's still asleep I'll be able to scoff you all to myself," A massive hand came hurtling down towards them.

"Run!" screamed Thumble Tumble, grabbing a hold of McCools' scarf. She pulled him with her as she raced off.

Sam had somehow managed to overtake them and was already standing at the broom with one hand on the handle, gripping the map tightly in the other.

"Get on!" he shouted urgently.

Thumble Tumble launched McCools through the air and he landed on the broom right in front of Sam.

The giant, who was called, Ralph, was smashing the ground with his fist, trying to swat Thumble Tumble as she sprinted towards them.

The vibrations sent her hurtling through the air and she landed right beside the broom. She jumped on. "Ferry Port," she panted.

Nothing happened.

"Ferry Port!" she shouted as loudly as she could. The broom hovered off the ground for a spilt second then fell back down, letting out a splutter as it landed.

"We're out of broom powder," McCools gasped, fumbling in his scarf.

Just as he managed to pull out the small pouch of broom powder from his scarf, the giant grabbed hold of the back of the broom and frantically swung it in the air, sending its three passengers hurtling off.

Sam landed head-first in the dirt. McCools bounced down beside him. Thumble Tumble was thrown high into the branches of a tree where she was left dangling helplessly by the hem of her dress. The giant lumbered towards her smacking his lips and stretched out his hand to grab her, when suddenly Smidge came flying out of nowhere.

"Oi, leave her alone," the tiny bird chirped.

The giant glanced at Smidge for a second, shrugged his shoulders and continued to reach for Thumble Tumble.

"Big Foot," squawked Smidge. "I'm talking to you."

The giant turned and started running towards Smidge. "Nobody calls me Big Foot," he roared.

Smidge flew into the trees with the giant chasing behind him.

Thumble Tumble tugged and pulled on her dress until she managed to wriggle free from the branch falling to the ground.

As she landed, she looked up to see a huge puff of orange smoke rise into the sky. It was coming from the direction in which Smidge had flown. There was an eerie silence in the air, then Smidge came flying back through the trees with a huge grin on his face.

"What happened?" gasped Thumble Tumble.

"Oh, he ran into a tree," Smidge smiled smugly.

Thumble Tumble smiled back at him warily, wondering to herself what had really happened in the trees!

Chapter 8

The Oarsmen

The 'giant' encounter had set them back a full hour. It was ten minutes to midnight, and they were stranded at the top of the Giant Hills.

"We'll never make it without a broom," sighed Sam.

"I'm afraid I have to agree," nodded McCools. "The only way to get to the Ferry Port on time is to fly."

Thumble Tumble jumped to her feet. "That's right, but there's more than one way to fly," she exclaimed excitedly. "Trust me on this. You have to do exactly what I do." She threw herself down on the ground and began rolling down then hill.

"Quickly!" she urged the others, before disappearing down the hill.

McCools tipped sideways and instantly sped down the hill, rolling past Thumble Tumble like a giant whizzing fur ball.

Sam lay down with hands above his head before rolling down the hill, whilst Smidge flew ahead to the Ferry Port.

After a few moments, all three of them had crashed

into the gates of Lochranza Castle. Thumble Tumble jumped to her feet and ran to the edge of the loch.

"Jock," she called into the water's surface.

A few little ripples started to appear, followed by a massive surge of water which exploded upwards as a huge purple dragon flew out of the loch up into the sky.

The magnificent beast came soaring back down and landed as softly as a marshmallow beside them.

"Good to see you Thumble Tumble?" the huge Sea Dragon roared. "But what are you doing here at this time of night?"

"We need to get to the Ferry Port by midnight. Thumble Tumble babbled breathlessly. "Can you get us there on time?"

"No problem," smiled Jock. "We've got a full five minutes. I'll get you there in three!" He laid his long tail out on the ground for them to use to walk onto his back. Thumble Tumble and McCools quickly walked up and sat down between the spikes that ran down the Sea Dragon's back. Sam watched from the side of the loch with his bottom jaw hanging open.

"Come on," Thumble Tumble called down, waving him to come onto the dragon's back.

Sam just gawked up at her.

"Snap out of it," she hollered, waving her wand. She sent a spray of tiny sparks towards him. They were exploding in front of his eyes, but Sam didn't budge. Then one tiny spark flew up his nose before popping. Sam sprung back to life.

"Are you kidding me?" he cried up to her. "That's a *dragon*!" he yelled, pointing at Jock.

"Well observed!" she replied. "A very friendly dragon

with really big wings. So, if you ever want to see your friends again, I suggest you get on. This dragon is the only chance we've got of making it to the Ferry Port on time."

Although it went against every instinct in his body, Sam walked up Jock's tail onto his back. As soon as Sam sat down Jock took off, flying through the air like a tornado.

The wind was icy cold, battering against their bodies as they soared through the night sky. They could barely open their eyes as they travelled almost at the speed of light across the island.

Jock stopped suddenly, jerking his passengers from their seats so that the three of them fell head-first into a waiting ship at the side of the Ferry Port – just as the final stroke of midnight chimed out from the port clock.

"Cutting it fine," came a ghostly voice from the back of the ship. Mogdred floated out from the shadows. "Do you have the map?"

"That we do," announced Sam, clutching the map tightly with both hands.

"Hmm. What do you think of your ship?" she asked, sweeping her hand out.

"Where are the sails?" quizzed Sam.

"Oh, you don't need sails for this journey," she hissed. "Where you're going there is no wind." She let out a hideous cackle clapped her hands once and started to chant: "Oarsmen of the deep, I awaken you from your sleep."

A grey mist gathered around the ship and it began rocking from side to side.

Sam peered over the side, then lurched back in horror. "What kind of magic is this?" he shouted.

Thumble Tumble stood transfixed as a dozen skeletons rose up out of the mist. Ten of them were wearing eye patches and at least four had peg legs. Several of them had large gold hoops hanging from where an ear lobe would have once been, and all of them had been branded on their left arms with the imprint of a skull-and-crossbones.

Jock, who had been watching from the sky above, came swooping down, spraying the deathly pirate crew with a massive water jet that knocked every one of them back into the murky waters.

"Call off your mutt!" shrieked Mogdred. She was standing mid-ship, holding McCools in the air with her sharp fingernail pointing directly into his temple.

"He's not a mutt," Thumble Tumble retorted.

"You fool," Mogdred spat back at her. "How do you expect to get this ship to World's End without any oarsmen?"

Thumble Tumble scowled at Mogdred. "He's not a mutt!" she repeated defiantly.

"Very well, call off your dragon," said Mogdred.

"He's not a pet either," seethed Thumble Tumble.

"Do *not* test me, child," Mogdred replied sternly. And she pushed her fingernail further into McCools' temple.

"Let them be," Thumble Tumble shouted up to Jock.

Jock bowed his head in acknowledgment of Thumble Tumble's request, but he continued circling in the sky above them.

The twelve skeletons re-emerged from the mist and started climbing up the ropes hanging over the side of the ship. The skeletons stood in two rows of six, facing one another.

Mogdred threw McCools onto the deck, then floated

between the two rows of skeletons, sprinkling each of them with red dust. "Oars!" she shrieked.

As she spoke each of the skeletons ripped off their right arm. They pointed the arms towards the side of the ship they were standing beside and the hands at the end of the arms each tore a hole in the side of the ship and slipped through. As the arms slipped through the holes, they transformed into long grey oars.

"As you have the map, you shall be the captain," she said, pointing to Sam.

The skeleton crew turned their heads towards Sam. Their blank gazes landed on him as they bellowed out in unison, "Aye, aye, Captain."

"Pick up your oars," Sam hollered.

The skeletons each picked up an oar.

"Reverse thrust and turn," Sam ordered. To which the skeletons began rowing backwards, and the ship slowly reversed away from the dock. When it fully detached from the dock the ship spun one hundred and eighty degrees, facing away from the Ferry Port.

"Good luck," said Mogdred. She then disappeared into a puff of smoke. "You'll need it," her voice trailed off in a wicked cackle.

"Full thrust ahead," Sam called out to the oarsmen.

The ship picked up speed as it left the port. Jock followed overhead until they were several miles out to sea.

"I don't think it will be safe to take your dragon where we're going," Smidge whispered into Thumble Tumble's ear. "A lot of people are still afraid of dragons and would kill him first, ask questions later," he continued with a concerned look in his eyes.

"I know," Thumble Tumble replied glumly.

"Jock," she shouted up, beckoning him to come closer.

"I don't think it's safe for you to come with us," she said gently, stroking his huge purple head.

"I don't care. I'm not leaving you," Jock replied, pulling away from her.

Smidge fluttered over and perched on Thumble Tumble's shoulder. "It's not safe for any of us if you come" he twittered.

"People fear dragons, so they'll try to kill you. If Thumble Tumble tries to help you, they'll end up killing her too!

So, you see, it's not just your life you're risking, you're risking her life too." He placed his head against Thumble Tumble's cheek.

"I hadn't thought about it like that," said Jock, with a huge lump in his throat. "I'd never put Thumble Tumble at risk."

"I know you wouldn't," Smidge continued in his sympathetic tone. "So probably best you head back now."

Jock nodded, and a single tear started to roll down his cheek.

"Please don't be sad," said Thumble Tumble. "Besides, I really need to let my aunts know what's happened – they'll be worried sick."

"Okay," he replied, looking slightly less gloomy.

"I'll head back to Arran and tell them what's happened. They'll know what to do."

Jock flew up into the sky with a single swoosh of his tail and disappeared in a flash.

"Are you okay?" McCools asked Thumble Tumble noticing her eyes were once again red.

"Yes, I'm fine," she fibbed.

Sam was standing at the helm. "Smidge, I think you should head up to the crow's nest as look-out," he said directing the little bird to the top mast of the sailless ship. Smidge reluctantly flew off Thumble Tumble's shoulder and up towards the crow's nest.

"McCools, you're probably best placed to read the map. It looks like complete gibberish to me!" Sam continued, spreading the map out on a small table beside the ship's wheel.

"And as captain, I'll steer!" he added gleefully, taking hold of the wheel.

"What about me?" asked Thumble Tumble, looking a little dismayed.

Sam paused momentarily then replied, "You'll be the cook. Every ship needs a cook."

"But the only thing I know how to make is Scoffalicious Chocolate," Thumble Tumble moaned.

"Then you'll make an excellent cook," said McCools. "And we'll all get to feast on our favourite food!"

Thumble Tumble beamed back at him, as they sailed off into the unknown.

Chapter 9

Witches Cove

McCools had been studying the map for several hours without uttering a single word.

"Do you think he can read it?" Sam whispered to Thumble Tumble, who was now busy preparing a big pot of Scoffalicious Chocolate in the kitchen.

"I'm pretty sure he'll work it out," she replied, stirring vigorously.

"It's just that we've been sailing in the same direction for seven hours," said Sam with a worried expression on his face.

Smidge flew though the open porthole into the kitchen. "Are you two thinking what I'm thinking?" he squawked.

"It depends what you're thinking, Smidge," replied Thumble Tumble, stroking the little bird's mohawk with her index finger.

Smidge shook her finger off. "That the Haggis hasn't got a clue where we are or where we're going!" he trilled, flapping his wings frantically.

Just then McCools walked into the kitchen, flattening

the little bird behind the kitchen door as it swung open.

"Something smells good," he smiled, unaware of Smidge sliding down the wall behind the kitchen door onto the floor.

"It's Scoffalicious Chocolate," grinned Thumble Tumble, picking the spoon out of the pot and handing it to McCools for a lick.

McCools took the spoon, and as he did so a huge dollop of chocolate fell off. The chocolate dollop landed slap bang on top of Smidge, who had only just managed to stand up after being crushed behind the door. He was now covered head to toe in thick, creamy chocolate.

"Delicious," said McCools, smacking his lips and taking another lick of the spoon. "The best dandelion cookies I've ever tasted."

"Dandelion flavoured chocolate?" Sam said inquisitively.

"Only for McCools," smiled Thumble Tumble. "Scoffalicious Chocolate tastes like your favourite food. Try it," she said reassuringly, holding out the pot.

Sam dipped his finger into the pot of chocolate and took a lick. "Cabbage and potatoes," he spluttered in disbelief. "And they taste just like how my mum used to make them."

"Enough chat about food," squawked Smidge, wiping the Scoffalicious Chocolate off his beak with his wing.

"Have you worked out what the symbols on the map mean yet?"

"Of course I have!" replied McCools.

"Well then, why haven't you given us any directions?" Smidge chirped angrily.

"Because we're already travelling in the right

direction," replied McCools, taking another spoonful of Scoffalicious Chocolate out of the pot. "We sail towards the North Star for two days, one hour and seventeen minutes, then we head towards Orion's Belt."

McCools paused to take a lick of chocolate off his spoon. Smidge scowled.

McCools dabbed his mouth with a tissue, then continued. "We follow Orion's Belt until we cross the path of a shooting star. When the star is overhead, we turn one hundred and seventy-eight degrees and we should arrive at Witches Cove within a day."

"Witches Cove," squawked Smidge, almost choking on his words. "Why are we going to that deathly place?"

"We need to pick up a special compass," McCools replied cagily.

"By pick up, you mean steal – don't you?" Smidge tweeted.

"You can't read the map! You're taking us to Witches Cove to get 'The Eye' to help you read the map – aren't you?" he demanded furiously.

"Yes," McCools replied sheepishly. "We've not actually started our journey to the end of the world yet. In order to get there, we need the Witches' Eye to let us read the map."

Thumble Tumble and Sam both looked startled.

"I didn't want to worry you," he pleaded.

"You should have told us where we are going," Thumble Tumble said, shaking her head in disappointment.

"I know," said McCools with his head held low.

"Oh well, we're on our way now so no real damage caused," she piped up, smiling at him.

"I agree," said Sam, licking another dollop of chocolate

from his finger.

"Well, I don't," Smidge fumed. "He's a liar!"

McCools chose to ignore Smidge's comments and instead took another large spoonful of chocolate from the pot.

"Brilliant," Smidge muttered, glowering at McCools. "We're all heading to Witches Cove, for a fate worse than death, and you three are just filling your faces with chocolate!"

He flew out of the kitchen porthole in a rage.

Thumble Tumble, McCools and Sam sat down around the kitchen table and continued tucking into generous portions of Scoffalicious Chocolate.

The next two days passed extremely slowly as there was very little for any of them to do.

McCools couldn't read the map without The Eye, and the ship pretty much sailed itself with the skeleton crew rowing around the clock. Thumble Tumble had already made enough Scoffalicious Chocolate to last them a month, and Smidge continued his huff by remaining in the crow's-nest.

They arrived at Witches Cove early in the morning. There was a chill in the air with a light mist gently floating on the ground. The land looked barren with no sign of vegetation or animal life anywhere.

In the distance they could see a trail of smoke drifting up into the sky.

"Do you think that's where The Eye is?" asked Thumble Tumble.

"I do," McCools answered uneasily.

"What's wrong?" quizzed Sam, sensing McCools' tension.

"According to stories, the Witches should be right here beside the shore," McCools replied. He then read aloud from an old scroll be produced from his scarf. "*Weary travellers must beware. Step on land, if you dare. When you reach this place by oar, Witches are watching from the shore.* So the Witches should be close by!" he exclaimed.

Smidge came flying down from the crow's nest for the first time in two days.

"They don't actually need to be at the shore to see you," he chirped. "You're obviously not as smart as you think!" he continued in a self-righteous tone.

"Witches Cove is home to three loathsome Witches. They were banished here hundreds of years ago by the Witch Council because of their appetite for children."

Thumble Tumble lurched back in horror.

"And it wasn't just human children," Smidge continued solemnly. "They ate all types of children. Pixies, Elves, Trolls and even Witches! They believed that by eating children they could stay young and beautiful forever. After they were banished, without access to children to dine on, they quickly aged and turned into the ugly old hags they really were. They were so ugly they couldn't bear to look at themselves, or each other so they gouged out their own eyes, retaining just one between them. The Eye has the power to see whatever the holder wishes. And the Witches always want to see fresh meat, so they'll be watching us right now."

Sure enough, the three Witches were sitting in a cave huddled together around a fire with a cauldron bubbling in the flame. They were passing The Eye between them as though they were playing a game of pass the parcel. As each of them took The Eye, they would burst into a shriek

of laughter, describing what they were going to do to the unsuspecting visitors.

"I'm going to dice the child up into a nice stew, with the orange puffy thing as dessert. You two can have the skinny one and the bird!" the first Witch cackled loudly.

"Give me The Eye," the second Witch wailed as she snatched the eye out of the first Witch's hands. "I'll grill the girl with some Goblin salad on the side. I'm not even sure if the orange puffy thing is edible!" she snorted. "And as for the bird..."

"My turn!" squealed the third Witch, almost dropping The Eye into the boiling cauldron as she grabbed it.

"I'll eat the child raw," she slobbered baring her sharp

pointy teeth. "You two can do what you want with the others," she said waving her hand as though the others were worthless.

"What if they don't come?" the first Witch suddenly announced in a panicked voice.

"Oh, they'll come," the third Witch whispered in a chilling tone, rubbing The Eye against her wrinkly cheek. The Eye has shown me that that they're coming to steal it!"

"Steal our Precious!" the other two Witches shrieked in unison.

"Don't worry, Precious," the third Witch said in baby talk, mollycoddling The Eye. "We won't let those nasty trespassers take you. We'll gobble them up as soon as they get close enough for us to grab them!"

"And if we can't catch them, we'll set Freeska on them," the second Witch added gleefully.

Freeska rose up from a pile of bones when she heard her name being used. "Meaow," she roared, shaking all six heads at once.

"Shhh," chorused the Witches together. "Be still, my pet. Your fresh bones will be here soon."

Freeska lay back down on her bed of crushed bones and began licking her paws in preparation.

Chapter 10

The Eye

Thumble Tumble, McCools and Smidge headed ashore. They decided it wouldn't be a good idea for all four of them to leave the ship. Sam remained on board as he was the captain – and so that there would be less chance of the skeleton crew rowing away without them.

"When we're in the Witches' lair, *do not* get too close to them," tweeted Smidge, as they made their way towards the trail of smoke. "They are devious creatures who'll try to trick us, and if they get a hold of you, they'll pop you straight into their cauldron, or even worse, their mouth!" He dangled his wing above his beak to illustrate.

Thumble Tumble gulped at the thought of being swallowed whole.

It wasn't long before they arrived at the mouth of a cave from which smoke was bellowing up through an opening in the roof. It was dark and damp inside the cave with dozens of massive stalactites climbing down from the ceiling.

Thumble Tumble took out her wand and uttered

"Luminata". A bright ray of light emerged from the tip her wand. As they walked further into the cave, they were overwhelmed by the smell of decaying bones.

"I thought there would be bats?" whispered Thumble Tumble.

"There used to be," Smidge replied ominously.

"Welcome, dear guests," a voice echoed off the dank walls. They could see a slight glow up ahead.

"Remember, not too close," Smidge tweeted quietly.

"Don't be afraid," the voice continued. "We are just three blind old hags. How could we possibly harm you?

"Yes, don't be afraid," a second voice cackled.

"Shut up," the first voice ordered. "I'm speaking to our guests."

"Who appointed you as spokesperson?" another voice interjected through the darkness.

The voices seemed to be coming from all directions.

"Get them," one of the Witches suddenly squealed. And from out of nowhere the three hags pounced.

The hags crashed and banged into one another as Thumble Tumble lifted her hologram spell.

"You tricked us," screamed one of the hags.

"Well, you did try to trick us," replied Thumble Tumble, still careful not to reveal her actual whereabouts.

"What do you want?" hissed the oldest of the three Witches, and as such deemed to have the most authority.

"We need to borrow The Eye," answered Thumble Tumble.

"Borrow!" the Witch lurched forward, grasping in the darkness. "Don't you mean *steal*?"

"We will return it," Thumble Tumble said confidently.

"And what will you give us in return for 'borrowing'

our Eye?" hissed the hag.

"Blood," replied Thumble Tumble. "Fresh blood!"

"We don't believe you," all three hags snarled together.

"Then have a taste," said Thumble Tumble, throwing a small vial towards them.

The eldest hag scrambled to the floor to feel for the vial with her hands.

"It's another trick," said one of the other hags. "Don't drink it. It's probably poison!"

The eldest hag opened the vial. "Let's find out," she shrieked, then poured the entire contents of the vial into the younger hag's mouth.

"No," squealed her unwilling candidate, clasping her hands around her throat. Then a moment later she began smacking her lips. "It's Troll blood," she announced excitedly. "Young Troll blood, my favourite!"

"Give it here," demanded the oldest hag, grabbing in the dark for the empty vial.

"There's plenty more where that came from," Thumble Tumble called out from the dark.

"What should we do?" the three Witches said in unison. They huddled tightly together and whispered frantically amongst themselves.

"Alright," the eldest Witch announced emerging from the huddle. "You can borrow The Eye. But first you must give us the blood."

"I don't think so," laughed Thumble Tumble. "You throw me The Eye and I'll throw you the blood at the same time."

"Very well," replied the hag. "On the count of three. One, two, three…" both parties threw their part of the bargain. Then the hag shouted out, "Freeska!"The giant feline jumped into action upon hearing her name. She scanned the cave with her perfect night vision.

"Yikes, I didn't see that coming," gasped Thumble Tumble as she caught The Eye in her hand.

"You two get to the entrance," shouted Smidge. "I'll distract it. All cats love birds!"

He flew directly between two of the giant cat's heads. Both heads lunged towards the tiny bird with jaws open wide. The beast let out an almighty roar as the two heads collided, then both slumped to the side, unconscious.

"Two down," Smidge tweeted to himself.

He spiralled in between three more heads. The heads twisted and turned, snapping at the cheeky little bird, until they'd tied themselves in a perfect bow.

"One left," Smidge sung out, taunting the creature.

Furious, it shook its tangled heads, trying to unravel them. Then a huge paw came crashing down on top of Smidge, but he was so small he just flew through the claws.

"Never mind the bird," hollered the hags. "Get The Eye." The huge feline took one final swipe at Smidge, then turned and started pounding towards the entrance of the cave.

"Hurry up!" Thumble Tumble called back to McCools.

McCools was a good ten yards behind her. He was hobbling as fast as his three legs could carry him. A huge whisker skimmed his backside. Then he shot up through the air. "Thrusterio!" called Thumble Tumble, just in time to lift McCools out of harm's way.

McCools hurtled through the air and landed on his head outside the cave. Thumble Tumble came racing out right behind him.

"Seal the cave," screamed Smidge as he flew towards them with Freeska literally a tongue's length behind him.

"Not until you're out," Thumble Tumble called back.

"Seal it now, or we'll all die," Smidge screeched.

She pointed her wand at the entrance: "Sealisio."

Her hand shook as she uttered the spell and a few small rocks began flying off the ground and sticking to the sides of the entrance. It made the entrance smaller, but it was still big enough for Freeska who was charging towards them with all six heads now awake and detangled.

"Quickly," Smidge squawked. He could feel Freeska's hot breath on his back.

"I'm not strong enough," gasped Thumble Tumble, still aiming her wand at the entrance.

"Use your ring," Smidge hollered as he flew out of the cave.

Freeska was only a few feet away from the entrance. Huge gobbets of saliva were flying out in all directions from her six sets of flapping jaws as she bounded towards them.

Thumble Tumble clasped her hands together and rubbed her ring. She took aim, dead centre of the cave entrance, then closed her eyes. Taking a deep breath, she shouted out "Sealisio."She slowly opened one eye, then gasped aloud. The cave entrance was still wide open.

They watched in terror for a split second as Freeska came charging out like a raging bull. There was a colossal crash as the huge beast smashed into the invisible force field which was now surrounding the cave entrance.

"It worked," Thumble Tumble called out in disbelief as she watched the massive cat claw at the force field, roaring in pain.

"Indeed it did," McCools smiled, dabbing the sweat away from his forehead.

"Let's get out of here," tweeted Smidge, looking flustered for the first time during the journey.

They hurriedly made their way back to the ship, where Sam ordered the oarsmen to row them to safety.

The three hags wailed in dismay. They could feel the pain of their pet's defeat.

"They've escaped," the eldest hag shrieked.

"But at least we still have the Troll blood," one of the other Witches cackled and she took a huge swig from the jar Thumble Tumble had thrown.

"Give it to me," the eldest Witch commanded grabbing the jar. She took a gulp then paused. "This isn't Troll blood. It's dwarf blood," she squealed with delight. "My favourite!"

The third Witch lurched over and snatched the jar. "Let me try."

When they were safely out of the cove Thumble Tumble walked to the back of the ship to cast one final spell. "Revealio!" she shouted at the top of her lungs, aiming her wand towards the cave.

Just then, the third Witch guzzled a huge helping from the jar. "Argh" she screamed, spitting the contents back into the jar.

"It's vile," she spluttered. "It tastes like chocolate," she continued, spitting.

The eldest Witch dipped her finger in the jar then rubbed it across her tongue. "It *is* chocolate" she declared. "The child Witch has deceived us once again."

"What shall we do?" the others cackled to their elder.

"She will not deceive us a third time," the eldest Witch

assured them.

"We made a pact. If she keeps her word and returns The Eye, she shall be spared. If she does not – she will DIE!"

"How can you be so sure?" asked the youngest Witch anxiously.

"I have sent the Guardian of The Eye. If Thumble Tumble betrays us, the Guardian will kill her!"

Chapter 11

The Map Awakens

McCools laid the map out on a table in the bridge. Now everyone could see that there was a hole in the centre of the map.

"I hope this works," he muttered, as he placed The Eye into the hole.

"Do you know what's meant to go in the hole?" squawked Smidge, inflating his chest to the size of a tennis ball.

"I know exactly what's meant to go in the hole," McCools replied sharply.

"The only problem is the item that belongs in the hole was destroyed by Mogdred."

"What should go in the hole?" asked Thumble Tumble, gazing at the map in dismay.

"The map is partner to the All Seeing Globe, but the globe was destroyed by Mogdred in a fit of rage. The globe was used to bring the map to life, revealing its hidden secrets. I thought that because The Eye has similar powers to the globe it might work in its place."

Thumble Tumble, McCools and Smidge all stared down at the map with The Eye now in its centre. Nothing had changed. It was still a round map with jagged lines evenly spaced around its circumference. In between each line there were strange symbols and letters that didn't make any sense at all.

"What's supposed to happen?" Thumble Tumble asked, breaking the silence.

"I'm not quite sure," replied McCools.

"Well, that's just perfect," squawked Smidge. "We're nearly eaten by a bunch of hags, then barely escape the clutches of their giant moggy, only to find out The Eye might not even work!"

He flicked his mohawk with his wing then swooshed out of the bridge.

"I was sure The Eye would work," said McCools, prodding it with his chubby finger. "It does pretty much the exact same thing as the All Seeing Globe."

"Perhaps there's a spell or something you're meant to say," said Thumble Tumble, examining the map more closely to see if she could find any clues.

She brushed her hand gently across its surface and as she did, the edge of her ring grazed The Eye. It opened immediately. The pupil darted from side to side, then it closed again.

"It's your ring," gasped McCools. "Touch it with your ring again." Thumble Tumble clenched her hand into a fist then tapped The Eye gently with her ring. The Eye opened once more, only this time the pupil was stationary. A purple fluid oozed over its iris, then poured out like tears. The fluid travelled along the jagged lines on the map, turning them into glowing rivers. Next, the symbols on the map started to move. They pieced together to create land masses, mountains and seas, with the letters assembling to form the names of the places. Finally, the places started to protrude from the map, with 3D images of mountains and islands rising up out of the map.

"That's where we need to go next!" exclaimed McCools, pointing to a fierce looking group of cliffs which pierced up out of the map like razors. Below them lay the words: *Crying Cliffs.*

"They look scary," said Thumble Tumble, placing her finger on the tip of the 3D image. "Ouch!" she squealed, as a bright red drop of blood appeared at the tip of her finger.

"Be careful," cautioned McCools, pulling her hand away. "Remember, the map is alive!"

Just then, Sam entered the bridge. "Wow, got the map to work!" he hollered, punching his hand in the air. "Where are we headed?"

"We need to get to these cliffs." McCools pointed at the map, being careful not to get too close.

"No problem," Sam tooted. "I'll go and set a course for the men... erm I mean... skeletons." Just as he was about to leave, he noticed some tiny splashes of colour around the cliffs on the map. It looked like little pink flowers blooming, then closing again.

"What are those?" he asked, mesmerised. "They look so pretty."

"They're anything but pretty," McCools said grimly, as he tapped Sam on the cheek to snap him out of his dreamy state.

"Those are the Sirens of the Dead Sea. Vile creatures that lure sailors to a murky death below the waves. They use their enchanting singing to hypnotise the sailors, then drag them to the seabed where they keep their bodies as trophies."

"Oh, I see," said Sam absentmindedly, still swaying from side to side to the singing he could hear inside his head.

McCools grabbed him by his arms and shook him. "Snap out of it," he shouted. Sam woke up from his trans looking confused.

"You need to be careful around the map," explained McCools. "It's alive, and so are all the things on it! I've not quite worked out how we're going to evade the sirens, but we've got a couple of days before we reach the cliffs, so I'm hoping we'll have thought of something before then."Sam nodded, then headed onto the deck to give the crew their new directions for the Crying Cliffs.

Chapter 12

The Crying Cliffs

The next day at sea passed without incidence. The ship sailed through the ocean without so much as a wobble. It was a completely different story the following day.

Smidge fluttered frantically between the bridge and the crow's nest to make sure they were still on course for the Crying Cliffs. Every now and then he'd swoop into the bridge and demand that Sam give him a progress report.

Sam stoically ignored him and continued steering the ship.

Then halfway through the afternoon the entire crew stopped rowing.

"What's going on?" Smidge screeched at the top of his tiny lungs. "Why aren't they rowing?"

"I don't know!" Sam shouted back at him. The blast of his voice almost sent Smidge tumbling overboard.

"We've entered the Dead Sea," McCools interposed. "The *dead* cannot *live* here," he continued in haunting tones. "Basically, our skeletons are dead again – so they can't row!"

"How are we supposed to get to the Crying Cliffs now?" Smidge screeched, his orange chest feathers almost turning red with fury. "We have no sails!"

"The tide will carry us to the Crying Cliffs," replied McCools. "It's not getting there I'm worried about, it's making it through them that's concerning me!"

Sure enough, the ship continued to travel at the same pace without the aid of its oarsmen, and by nightfall they could see the glimmering peaks of razor-sharp cliffs in the distance.

The moon was high in the sky, lighting up the sea below. It was three-quarters full.

McCools glanced at Thumble Tumble. "Only four more nights until it's full again," he said nervously.

"Don't worry," Thumble Tumble smiled. "We'll have delivered the key and be well out of Mogdred's clutches before then."

"I hope so," McCools replied. "We're almost there," he called out to Sam. "You'll need to navigate through the cliffs. Smidge will be your eyes from above and I'll lookout from the front."He then addressed Thumble Tumble. "You'll need to use your powers to slow us down. It's impossible to negotiate the cliffs at this speed."Everyone took their positions. Thumble Tumble was at the front with McCools. Sam was at the helm and Smidge was eagerly perched in the crow's nest.

Thumble Tumble took out her wand and pointed it towards the water. "Deceleratio!" she cried.

The ship started to slow down, although not enough to allow them to negotiate the cliffs.

"Deceleratio Maximus!" Thumble Tumble shouted again.

The ship's pace decreased somewhat, but they were still travelling too fast.

"I can't slow us down in time," she gasped. Just then a massive wave hit the front of the ship sending them hurtling across the deck.

McCools grabbed hold of one of the skeleton crewmate's feet, which promptly detached. He careered towards the back of the ship and crashed into the stern. A few seconds later, Thumble Tumble crashed into him.

She gripped hold of the side of the ship and pulled herself to her feet. Clutching on to steady herself, she aimed her wand again. "Deceleratio!" she said, with a look of determination on her face.

The spell still wasn't strong enough, and the ship continued careering through the choppy waters.

"We need sails," McCools shouted up from the deck, still unable to regain his balance as the ship torpedoed towards the deadly cliffs.

"Sails?" Thumble Tumble shouted back, confused. "Won't they just make us go faster?"

"There's no wind. They'll act like a parachute. Trust me!"

Thumble Tumble thrust her hand above her head. *"Where masts are clear let sails appear,"* she chanted.

Suddenly, two huge white sails started rolling down from the bare masts. As they dropped, they filled with air, instantly halving the ships speed. The sudden jerk sent McCools flying over the side of the ship. Thumble Tumble managed to grab his hand just before he disappeared into the murky water below them.

Sam took the wheel with both hands. "Which way?" he shouted up to Smidge.

"Port side," Smidge screeched back. Sam spun the wheel and the ship veered to the left, just missing the side of the first cliff.

"Now starboard" Smidge squawked. Sam pulled the wheel hard in the opposite direction and the ship swung round, skirting the edge of another razor-sharp cliff.

Rocks started rolling down from the cliffs, smashing onto the deck like a shower of tiny cannonballs.

"Stay clear of the sides," McCools hollered from the back of the ship. "Those rocks falling like teardrops are why they're called the Crying Cliffs."

Sam spun the wheel again, manoeuvring the ship away from the cliffs.

"Watch out," Smidge screamed down from the lookout.

Sam looked up to see two cliffs straddling a narrow strip of water. The cliffs were leaning in towards one another, with claw like spikes jagging out from their sides.

"I'll go around them," Sam shouted out, and he began spinning the wheel.

"We need to go through them to reach World's End," shouted McCools, who was now clambering across the deck to help Sam at the helm.

"Through them!" Sam gulped, as he swung the wheel back around directing the ship between the fierce looking cliffs. "I'm not sure the gap's wide enough."

McCools staggered up to the helm. "Neither am I, but this is the only way."

"Dead straight ahead," Smidge squawked down from the crow's-nest.

As he steered the ship between the cliffs, beads of sweat rolled from Sam's forehead into his eyes. He took one hand off the wheel for a split second to wipe his eyes and the ship veered towards the side of the cliff, they were bombarded by a torrent of rocks. The Crying Cliffs had begun to 'weep'. Sam grabbed the wheel and managed to pull the ship away from the cliffs. With a concentrated look on his face, he navigated through the narrow, winding channel for several nerve-racking miles. It was deathly quiet. Even the sea was silent.

"We're almost there," Smidge tweeted, breaking the eerie silence.

After a few more miles, the channel began to widen and the cliffs receded into the water. Sam carefully negotiated the last few peaks before they finally emerged back onto open seas.

"Well, that was easy!" Sam said sarcastically, feeling please with himself.

"Yes" mused McCools. "Perhaps a little bit too easy," he murmured to himself as he surveyed the sinister water surrounding them.

Chapter 13

Sirens of the Deep

The 'parachute' sails had deflated and were now lying on top of the water, gently bobbing up and down.

The fur on the back of McCools neck had gone rigid.

"Something feels wrong," he said, rubbing the fur to smooth it down.

"Don't be such a humbug!" trilled Smidge. "Well done, Sam," he shouted, flapping his wings together in applause. He twirled down towards the helm to congratulate Sam in person, but Sam wasn't there.

He was standing on the side of the ship, swaying from foot to foot. His eyes were glazed over, and he had a ridiculous grin on his face.

"It's the Sirens," shouted McCools. "They've enchanted him with their singing. Grab him!"

"With what?" Smidge retorted, flicking out his wings.

McCools sped towards Sam just as he stepped off the side. He fell feet-first into the water and sank like a brick.

Thumble Tumble heard the splash and came running. "Where's Sam?" she gasped.

"It's the Sirens," replied McCools. "They've enchanted him."

"I can't hear anything," said Thumble Tumble, straining her ears to listen.

"Their singing can't be heard by Witches, or haggis," said McCools. "And it would appear birds can't hear them either," he continued, throwing Smidge an accusing glance.

"Where are they taking him?" Thumble Tumble asked anxiously.

"They'll drag him to the bottom of the sea," McCools replied with a lump in his throat.

"We need to get to him before he drowns!" Thumble Tumble raced to the side of the ship and launched herself over. Just as she entered the water she called out "Mermac!" and thrust the tip of her wand into her stomach.

Water filled her lungs, choking her as she sank below the surface. She held her mouth closed instinctively so as not to take in water. Her legs felt numb and her vision was blurred. The pressure of the water was crushing her ribs and she let out an almighty sneeze. Bubbles shot out of her nose, down towards her feet. The fogginess cleared from her eyes and as she looked down instead of feet, she was greeted by a huge tartan tail. She gulped in water, startled at the sight of the magnificent tail, then realised she was breathing – underwater.

Thumble Tumble clumsily wagged her tail as she swam further into the depths of the stunning underwater world. In the distance she could see the vague silhouettes of three figures. Two with fish tails, and one in between them resembling a Goblin.

As she gained on them, one of the Sirens turned and

sprayed a haze of dark purple ink from its mouth. The creature, which had a human torso and fish tail, snarled at her, baring its claw-like teeth before flicking its tail and swimming back towards its partner.

The ink burned into Thumble Tumble's eyes, blurring her vision once more. She kept swimming deeper and deeper until she reached the seabed, where she managed to get tangled in long seaweed. She ripped at the seaweed to pull herself free, releasing a green liquid which acted like an antidote to the Siren's ink.

Her eyes darted from side to side trying to catch a glimpse of Sam and his captors, but all she could see was a variety of brightly coloured fish and crustaceans. She watched in wonder as a shoal of vivid blue fish swam past her, each of them with a little green flash that lit up their fins.

They were followed by a group of two-headed seahorses, each no bigger than her little finger. As the seahorses swam past, she caught a glimpse of one of the Sirens disappearing into a dense patch of seaweed.

She followed, taking care not to hit the seaweed with her tail. When she emerged at the other side Sam was right in front of her. He was floating upside down inside a wooden cage that was tied onto the seabed with long strands of seaweed. There was no sign of the Sirens.

Thumble Tumble glided through the water until she was under the cage. She used her wand to cut a hole in the bottom of the cage and swam in. Sam was floating, his eyes wide open. Thumble Tumble placed the tip her wand into his mouth and whispered, "Breath". Sam's body remained limp and unresponsive. His lungs were so full of water it was impossible for him to breathe. Thumble

Tumble could see the last glimmers of life flickering out. She placed her wand back in his mouth and blew gently. As she said the word "Freeziato", her icy cold breath sped through Sam, freezing his body. Thumble Tumble grabbed hold of him and swam to the bottom of the cage.

Just as she popped her head through the hole she had made there, both Sirens came charging towards her from different directions, their arms outstretched, each of them brandishing a dagger. Thumble Tumble pulled her head back just as one of the Sirens swiped at her.

The Sirens grinned up at Thumble Tumble as they circled below the cage, every so often lunging at her with their daggers. She tried to take a shot at them with her wand, but she was struggling to keep hold of Sam and take aim. But when one of the Sirens started to swim into the cage from below, Thumble Tumble managed to aim her wand. Just then, a shooting pain shot down her arm. The other Siren had crept up the side of the cage and stabbed her in the shoulder.

Thumble Tumble blasted the Siren below with her wand then screamed out in agony. Blood was pouring from her wound, sending a trail of red mist through the water.

The Sirens feasted their eyes on their two 'trophies'. They knew it would only be a matter of time before Thumble Tumble passed out from losing so much blood.

Her eyes had begun to flicker, and her head tilted forward. Sam's body was getting heavier with each drop of blood she lost.

The second her eyes finally closed, the Sirens reached into the cage to collect their trophies. At that very moment, the cage shot across the ocean floor, ripping free from the

long grass securing it to the seabed.

The Sirens scanned the sea around them to find out what had hit the cage. Suddenly, a massive grey shark came charging through the water. It was at least twenty feet long with a huge orange fin on its back. The shark's nose hit the cage, this time completely shattering it.

Thumble Tumble's eyes shot open. At once, she grabbed Sam and started swimming towards the surface. The Sirens sped after her, thrusting their daggers out in front of them. One lunged her dagger towards Thumble Tumble's tail just as the mammoth shark returned to swat both Sirens like flies. The pair of them crashed onto the seabed, screaming wrathfully as they watched their trophies swim to freedom.

At last, Thumble Tumble's head pushed through the surface of the water. As she emerged, she began coughing up water. After a few seconds she could feel herself breathing again. She hauled Sam's body to the side of the ship and McCools dragged him on board. Thumble Tumble hauled herself onto the ship. The second her tartan fishtail left the water it turned back into legs, complete with stripy tights and pink shoes.

Smidge appeared beside McCools. His feathers were drenched and he was full of complaints about how McCools had soaked him as he pulled Sam from the water.

"We need to defrost Sam," Thumble Tumble said, ignoring Smidge.

McCools and Smidge looked at one another blankly.

"He was about to drown, so I froze him," she explained with a worried expression.

"What a brilliant idea," beamed MCools. "But we've not got much time. You'll need to get him breathing again soon, or his lungs will be so rigid he won't be able to use them."Thumble Tumble looked back anxiously. "I don't have my wand. I lost it fighting the Sirens."

The three of them stared down at Sam's rigid body, then Thumble Tumble announced, "I think I know what might work." She rummaged in her dress pocket for a few seconds before pulling out a rusty old cup.

"Lazlo's Cup!" grinned McCools.

Thumble Tumble gently placed the cup against Sam's blue lips and began to pour. A dark yellow fluid flowed into his mouth. As soon as the fluid touched his tongue his body transformed from being rigid to totally limp.

"He's defrosted," announced McCools. "Help me turn him over."

They turned Sam onto his front and McCools jumped onto his back. Water gushed out of Sam's mouth and nose, but he still lay lifeless on the deck.

McCools leapt in the air to jump on him again, only this time he was met with Sam's thrusting hand.

"That's enough bouncing for one day," Sam managed to splutter before he coughed up the remaining sea water from his lungs.

Chapter 14

Fairy Island

Sam spent the next few hours below deck, recovering from his ordeal. The ship drifted without guidance, then just as the sun was setting on the horizon, the skeleton crew began to wake up.

One by one the oarsmen came to life, sitting bolt upright with a tight grip on their oars awaiting their orders.

"We must have left the Dead Sea," said McCools, delighted to have the oarsmen back.

McCools took the helm and called out directions, but the crew didn't budge.

Thumble Tumble went below deck to find Sam, who was now feeling much better. So much so, he was sitting in the kitchen tucking into a huge bowl of Scoffalicious Chocolate.

"We need you on deck," she called out, as she poked her head into the kitchen.

"Why me?" Sam muffled through a mouthful of chocolate.

"You're the captain," she nodded, giving him a little

salute. "So, you'd better polish off that chocolate pronto and head on deck. Unless of course you fancy drifting back towards the Sirens?"

Sam almost choked on his chocolate. "No thank you," he spluttered and jumped to his feet.

"Where too?" he panted, still catching his breath after bolting up the stairs to the upper deck.

"Fairy Island," replied McCools. "Our final destination!"

"I thought our final destination was Worlds End!" said Sam, looking puzzled.

"It is" relied McCools. "Fairy Island is Worlds End!"

"It sounds really nice," said Thumble Tumble, clapping her hands excitedly. "Yes, if you like being hung upside down and dipped in water until you disintegrate," Smidge chirped.

"Oh, don't be so dramatic," said McCools. "That's only if you're a Night Witch, which Thumble Tumble is not!"

"Why do the fairies hate Night Witches so much?" asked Thumble Tumble. "I mean, apart from the obvious reasons – that they are loathsome creatures, hell bent on destruction." McCools cleared his throat. "A number of years ago, Mogdred visited Fairy Island looking for a special cauldron.

"The Cauldron of Undry!" Thumble Tumble butted in.

"Yes" nodded McCools. "But when the Fairy Queen said she didn't have the cauldron, Mogdred didn't believe her. So as a punishment for not giving up the cauldron, Mogdred placed a dark enchantment over the island.

"What made Mogdred think the cauldron was on Fairy Island?" asked Thumble Tumble.

"There are lots of magical items hidden on Fairy Island," replied McCools. Because of its isolated location beyond the Crying Cliffs, many creatures from the magical realm hide their enchanted possessions there. "

"Ah, so that's why we're going," Thumble Tumble said, nodding to herself. "The key to Medusa's chest is hidden there."

"Well, it is according to the map," replied McCools. "Let's just hope the Fairy Queen is willing to give it to us."

"What do you mean?" piped up Sam. "I thought we could just take the key."

"Not exactly," said McCools, shaking his head. "We'll need to barter for it. The Queen doesn't like to part with a magical treasure unless she is given something of equal value to replace it!"

"What do we have of equal value to the key?" Smidge tweeted.

"I'm afraid we'll just need to cross that bridge when we come to it," replied McCools.

"Well you *should* be afraid," Smidge chirped in a high pitch tone.

"The Fairy Queen can be a very nasty piece of work if crossed. Just look at what she does to Night Witches!"

Thumble Tumble, McCools and Sam each stared at one another, perplexed by Smidge's comments.

"I mean, if she can disintegrate Night Witches, I'm sure she can think of something equally gruesome for us," Smidge added.

"It can't be any worse that what those vile Sirens had planned for me, so let's get a move on," Sam said.

"The island only reveals itself on one night of the year,"

said McCools. "And coincidentally that night happens to be tonight."

"At sunset the island lights up under a magical display of fireworks. It only lasts for a few seconds and when it's over the island is covered in a veil of fairy dust, making it completely undetectable for another full year."

"What are the coordinates?" asked Sam.

"North-west for 7,000 nautical miles," answered McCools.

Sam hollered the directions, and within seconds the oarsmen were in full swing. The ship ploughed through the ocean, creating a mini tidal wave in its wake.

It didn't take the skeleton crew long to reach their destination.

When Sam shouted "Halt!" they instantly raised their oars. The ship came to an abrupt stop, sending Sam flying over the ships wheel. Smidge came tumbling down from his perch and landed on top of his head.

"I take it we've arrived," he squawked in his usual angry tone.

"Yes" Sam shouted back, as he picked himself up off the deck. "And thankfully we're on time," he continued, pointing up at the sun, which was still high in the sky.

Chapter 15

Queen of the Fairies

Thumble Tumble stood back to back with Sam and McCools on the ship's deck, with Smidge fluttering around her head. They were looking up at the sky in all directions to make sure they didn't miss the fairy fireworks.

They watched intently as the sun gradually disappeared over the horizon. It looked just like a giant yellow cookie being dipped into an enormous cup of tea, thought McCools, licking his lips. When the last remaining slither of sunlight disappeared, they were plunged into complete darkness.

"Nothing's happening!" squawked Smidge.

"Just keep looking," snapped McCools.

They stood staring into the darkness, with the ship gently swaying. The motion made them feel strangely calm.

Sam leaned down to pick up a lantern.

"Not yet," whispered McCools, and he signalled to Sam to stand back up.

Now they could hear a soft popping sound as though

someone was making popcorn far away, but there was still no sign of any fireworks.

The popping started to get louder and closer together until it sounded like a continuous series of mini-explosions. Suddenly, a gash of light tore through the darkness. It looked as though someone had slashed through the sky's skin, revealing its bright pink flesh. Glistening pink light poured out of the scar, reflecting off the sea like twinkling stars. The light coming from the scar started to weave its way across the sky, changing colour as it moved. The pink morphed into violet, which then changed to electric blue before turning green.

"So, these are fairy fireworks!" Thumble Tumble said in awe, mesmerised by the stunning display.

"Yup," McCools grinned back.

The bright green light started to fade, dowsing the twinkling stars back into the sea.

"There it is!" shouted Sam, pointing to a tiny clump in the distance.

He scrambled below deck, reappearing seconds later brandishing a small brass telescope.He fumbled clumsily trying to open the telescope
. "Hurry up," Smidge squawked.

"I'm going as fast as I can," Sam replied, still scrabbling with the telescope.

Thumble Tumble grabbed the end of the telescope and pulled. It immediately extended to its full length. "There you go!"

Sam put the telescope to his eye, licked his index finger and stuck it in the air. "North by North-west" he shouted out, relieved there was some moonlight to see by.

As soon as he called out the coordinated, the light in

the sky went out, once again plunging them into darkness.

Thumble Tumble picked up the lantern by Sam's foot and said "Illuminati!" with her eyes closed, hoping the spell would work without the aid of a wand. It flickered momentarily then burst into flame lighting up the whole deck.

Sam took the wheel and set course for Fairy Island.

The island didn't look anything like Thumble Tumble expected. She had imagined it would be crammed full of vibrant flowers, rainbows and waterfalls. Instead, they arrived on a desolate shore where the closest thing to flowers were dreary brown weeds, and in place of waterfalls there were muddy puddles surrounded by obnoxious-looking toads."This is a result of Mogdreds evil enchantment," said McCools.

"She cursed the fairies so they couldn't fly and so they became sad. The thing about fairies is that when they become sad, everything around them becomes sad too. Flowers stop blooming and waterfalls cease to flow. Eventually, everything of beauty dies."

"No wonder they don't like Night Witches," said Sam.

"Oh, boo hoo," tweeted Smidge. "We're not here to get all emotional over a bunch of fairies. We're on a mission… or have you all forgotten about your friends held captive back on Arran?"

Sam threw Smidge an angry glare.

"That's enough," McCools interjected. "I hate to say it, but Smidge is right. We have to get a move on, for all our sakes. The Queen's castle is on the other side of the forest," he said, pointing in the direction of a spooky mass of trees.

As they got closer, they discovered that the forest was

surrounded by a deep layer of thorn bushes. Like all the other plants on the island, they were bare of leaves making their scalpel like thorns all the more dangerous.

"How are you lot going to get through that?" chirped Smidge.

"We don't," shrugged McCools. "We'll have to walk around it."

It was a long trek round the thorn bushes and it took them several hours to reach the entrance to the Fairy Queen's castle, which had eight turrets, two on each corner, all sitting at different heights. The formerly magnificent towers, which had once been coloured in vibrant tints of gold and orange, were now varying shades of grey, grim as the surrounding landscape.

Before Mogdred's enchantment, the turrets had been covered in rubies and emeralds that were famous for creating a magnificent rainbow that sat over the castle. Now the only thing sitting over the castle was an aura of gloom.

Two imposing iron gates barred the way into the castle. There was no sign of the hanging vines that once used to greet visitors by hugging them before they entered.

McCools approached the gates and gently ran his stubby digits across the metal. Slowly, they began to creak open."Come on," he beckoned the others.

The gates closed behind them with a loud clink.

"I don't like this place," Smidge whinged.

Inside, the castle was just as gloomy as outside. The entrance was a large hexagonal room, with long dark passageways leading away from each of its sides. Above them, the ceiling was made of glass through which they could see a bright blue sky.

"Beautiful, isn't it?" came a whimsical voice from the passageway on their immediate left. "Just a shame all it acts as is a reminder that we can no longer fly."The voice belonged to a little fairy, no more than eight inches tall. She had long hair that was bunched on top of her head in three swooshing pony tails. Her skin was a dull purple, with a rash of tiny red dots all over her face, arms and legs. There were two paper-thin wings attached to her back and these too were purple with red dots. She was wearing a brown dress made from a single oak leaf and her feet were bare.

"Long time no see, McCools," she smiled, before rushing

forward and wrapping her arms around McCools' middle.

"So good to meet you, Queen Ruby," said Thumble Tumble, with a little curtsy.

The fairly let out a little giggle, which Thumble Tumble thought was rather rude!

Sam stepped forward to take a bow, at which point the little fairy burst into a fit of laughter.

"I'm not the Queen," she giggled.

Both Sam and Thumble Tumble looked towards McCools with disapproving frowns, but he was bent over with laughter.

"I'm sorry," he chuckled. "This is Violet, the Queen's younger sister. This wee scoundrel loves to read, so she used to visit me to use my library. Well, to be precise, she broke into my library, but then realised she didn't need to sneak in and pinch my books as they were all available for her to borrow," he smiled.

"So, you knew the Fairy Queen all along," Smidge tweeted angrily.

"No" replied McCools. "In fact, I've never met her."

"Well you're meeting me now," came a voice from behind them.

They spun round to find another tiny fairy standing before them. She was a carbon copy of her younger sister, with red skin covered in purple dots. Slightly taller than Violet, she also had long hair which was tied in a plait that hung over her left shoulder and dropped down to her waist.

"We rarely have visitors to Fairy Island these days, so I'm guessing you've come here to get something?" Her tone was polite, but cold.

"We're looking for the key to Medusa's chest," Thumble Tumble answered.

"Well, that I can give you, but what will you give me in return?" said the Fairy Queen, pacing in front of her guests.

She suddenly stopped and stared directly at Thumble Tumble's hand.

"I thought I could see an aura around you," she said, gesturing to Thumble Tumble's ring. "You are the Protector. I've heard many stories about you already – and you're still only a child! They say you're destined to destroy Mogdred."

"Only if she doesn't kill me first," Thumble Tumble laughed nervously.

The Queen allowed herself a miniscule smile. "Protector or not, my terms are clear. I shall give you the key if you have a treasure of equal value for me."

"We have The Eye," Smidge butted in.

"That would be suffice," replied the Queen.

"I promised we would return The Eye," Thumble Tumble protested, glaring at Smidge.

"Yes, and they promised they wouldn't try to eat us, but that was a lie," he retorted.

"Do you have anything else?" asked the Queen.

Thumble Tumble looked towards McCools, hoping he'd come up with something.

"We have the Lazlo Cup," he announced.

"It is magical" replied the Queen. "But not as precious as the key to Medusa's chest. Unless you have something else to offer me, I'm afraid we do not have a deal."

She turned on her heels and started to walk back along the dark passage.

"My ring!" shouted Thumble Tumble. "I'll give you my ring."

The Queen spun round, flicking her long plait back

over her shoulder. "Excellent!"

"You can't trade your ring," McCools pleaded.

"I have to. I made a deal with the Witches. And I'm *no liar*," she added, staring at Smidge.

"I will tell you where you can find the key, and when you have it, you can give me the ring – deal?" said the Queen, holding out her hand.

Thumble Tumble shook the Queen's hand with a heavy heart.

"The key is hidden under a lily pad on Critter's Pond," said the Queen.

"Critter's Pond," gasped Violet. "It's way too dangerous – they can't go there."

"Be quiet," the Queen ordered.

"Where is it?" asked Sam, sounding concerned.

"It's in the centre of the Forest of Thorns," the Queen replied. "I don't deny that it won't be easy to retrieve, but Thumble Tumble has defeated Mogdred, so if anyone can bring back the key – it's her."

Chapter 16

The Forest of Thorns

Queen Ruby escorted them to the edge of the forest with Violet in tow. The whole way there she kept squeezing McCools' hand.

"I know it's dangerous," he sighed. "But we need to get that key. Our friends' lives are depending on it!"

"You don't understand," she whispered.

"What doesn't he understand?" the Queen said sharply, cutting into their private conversation.

"Nothing," Violet replied sheepishly.

The Queen placed her finger against the wall of thorns and drew the outline of a small entrance. She then took some sparkly dust out of her pocket and threw it at the outline, uttering the words "Enterous Maximus". The thorns inside the outline disappeared, creating a small hole which instantly quadrupled in size to reveal a path inside the forest.

"Follow the path to the middle of the forest and that's where you'll find Critter's Pond," the Queen said. Her voice took on an intensely serious tone. "But be very careful, as *nothing* is what it seems inside the forest."

"Is that it?" chirped Smidge. "Is that all the guidance the great Queen of the Fairies can provide?"

"Fairies can no longer enter the forest," the Queen replied solemnly. "Ever since Mogdred placed her evil curse over our island we have been unable to set foot in the forest. Any fairy who does, turns to dust! What I can tell you, is that the forest used to be surrounded by stunning rose bushes, but now only thorns pierce through where rose petals once bloomed. Like so many beautiful things on our island, the forest turned ugly after the curse, and so did the creatures inside. Some of them mutated into hideous monsters, so we don't know what horrors you may face."

"That's comforting," tutted Smidge, rolling his eyes.

"Smidge, if you're that worried, why don't you just stay here with Ruby and Violet?" suggested Thumble Tumble.

"I'd rather take my chances in the forest," he chirped cheekily, then he flew through the entrance. Thumble Tumble walked through after Smidge, followed by McCools and Sam, each of them drawing a deep breath as they took their first step across the threshold, as if expecting something terrible to happen.

"It all seems okay," said Thumble Tumble, giving the fairies a thumbs-up.

"Just remember, *nothing* is what it seems," the Queen reiterated.

They followed the path into the forest for thirty minutes without seeing or hearing another creature, before reaching a canyon. Thumble Tumble tipped her head over the side to see how deep it was, but the base was so far down she couldn't even see it.

"Wow, that's deep," she said, stepping back quickly.

She noticed a rickety old plank of wood that formed a makeshift bridge across the canyon.

"Do you think that's sturdy enough for us to walk across?" she asked the others.

"Let's find out," replied Sam, stepping forward.

"Stop!" shouted McCools. "Remember what Queen Ruby said about things not being what they seem?"

"Trust me," Sam smiled cockily. "I know a thing or two about walking across a plank!"

"But that's not a plank," McCools spluttered. He scooped up a handful of dirt and threw it onto the plank.

Immediately, what had seemed an inanimate plank of wood started coughing, revealing a cavernous mouth with huge teeth in its centre."You may as well open your eyes," said McCools. "I know you're a stick insect. A very big, very hungry, stick insect," he added.

"Very well," the creature replied, opening its seven eyes and shaking the dirt off its long body. They could now see that the giant stick insect was shackled to the sides of the canyon.

"How did you see me?" the insect enquired.

"I could see your third eye twitching," replied McCools.

"You seem like a clever fellow," said the insect. "So you will have guessed you have to cross me to get to the other side. And as you say yourself, I'm *very* hungry! But if you let me eat just one of you, I'll let the others pass."McCools had every appearance of seriously considering this offer. His companions stared at him in horrified disbelief.

"That seems like a fair deal," he replied after a few moments' thought. His friends' expressions transformed to shock at his response.

"On one condition," McCools added, raising his stubby index finger in the air.

"You must let three of us pass safely first, and then you can eat the fourth person."

"Agreed," replied the giant stick insect, licking his lips.

"I'll go first," announced McCools. He carefully placed one foot onto the insect. It closed its eyes and mouth. McCools popped his second, then third foot on and quickly hobbled across the insect's back to the other side of the canyon.

"Your next, Thumble Tumble," he shouted back across the twenty-foot wide canyon.

Thumble Tumble instinctively felt inside her pocket to get her wand, before remembering she'd lost it fighting the Sirens.

She stepped onto the insect, wobbled precariously, then ran as fast as she could straight across without looking down once.

Before anyone could say another word, Smidge flew over the canyon tweeting, "I'm afraid you're dinner, Sam!"

Sam stared across the canyon, dumbfounded by what had just happened.

"That is, of course, unless you no longer want to cross the canyon," McCools shouted across at him, winking.

"That's not fair," the massive insect hollered, reopening its giant mouth and all seven eyes.

"You said I could eat him," it yelled, tugging at its

shackles.

"I said you could eat the fourth person to cross," McCools corrected the insect. "It's not my fault the fourth person decided not to cross!"

"Good luck," waved Sam, then he turned on his heels and raced back along the path.

The others could still hear the stick insect's howls of fury and frustration as they made their way deeper into the forest. The path was two metres wide, fringed by spiky thorn bushes that clawed at their clothes and skin.

"I need a seat," puffed McCools.

"What's that?" quizzed Thumble Tumble, pointing at the little brown fence with steps on either side.

"It's a stile," replied McCools. "A type of gate that you have to climb over."

"Or fly over!" smirked Smidge, flying ahead.

"Watch out!" screamed Thumble Tumble.

Smidge looked down just in time to see the stile transform into a giant bat with slatted wings. He flicked in another direction and disappeared through a tiny hole in the thorny bushes. The massive bat flew after him, smashing through the bushes with its powerful wings.

"Hurry up!" McCools urged, grabbing Thumble Tumble's hand as he ran along the path.

"Smidge can take care of himself," he gasped. "We need to get to Critter's Pond!"

They didn't stop running until they came to a fork in the path, at which point McCools promptly keeled over, face first.

"It can't be much further," said Thumble Tumble. "You can do it," she encouraged him.

"Of course I can," McCools panted. "I was just

listening for the sound of water running underground," he continued, regaining his composure.

"Sorry?" giggled Thumble Tumble. "I thought you'd just collapsed from exhaustion."

McCools' eyes narrowed momentarily, before he burst out laughing. "Yes, that too," he grinned.

"We should follow the path on the left," he said with an air of confidence.

"Wow… is that because you could hear the water running under the path?" gasped Thumble Tumble, amazed by McCools' divining skills.

McCools shook his head. "I actually couldn't hear anything," he replied, still grinning. "But that sign is a bit of a giveaway." He nodded towards a wooden arrow pointing along the path to the right with the words: CRITTER'S POND carved on it.

"But the sign's pointing right," said Thumble Tumble, scratching her head.

"Exactly the reason why we should go left!" McCools insisted, setting off at cracking pace.

This path was scarier than the previous one. It was much narrower, and the thorn bush claws were much longer and even sharper. "Are you sure this is the correct path?" Thumble Tumble asked anxiously.

"I hope so," replied McCools, ducking to avoid being scalped by a thorn.

As he ducked, he noticed a miniscule frog on the path. The tiny frog was bright yellow with red stripes running down its back. In the dim light of the forest, its skin looked luminous. When it spotted McCools, its eyes almost popped out of its head and it started hopping backwards.

"Follow that frog," McCools shouted to Thumble

Tumble. "Where there's a frog, there's a pond!"

They chased after the little frog, not noticing that it was getting bigger as it hopped along. By they time they realised how large it had grown, it was too late! The frog stopped dead in their path and turned around. It was now twice the size of Thumble Tumble and its eyes were bulging out of its head like two inflated beach balls. The horrid creature was drooling copiously as it towered over them.

"Don't touch it," cautioned McCools. "It has poisonous skin."

"I'm not planning on touching it, but I'm not sure if the frog returns the sentiment," Thumble Tumble squealed. As she dived out of the way of the frog's webbed foot, she caught sight of the pond through the frog's legs.

"The pond is right behind it," she called to McCools, just as the frog took another swipe at her. "There's no way through," she gasped.The giant frog started moving towards them, cracking its neck from side to side to loosen its jaws.

"Do you think you can crawl under it?" McCools asked.

"Not without touching it," Thumble Tumble shook her head.

"Then we'll need a distraction," he said. "I want you to run as fast as you can and when I say dive you have to hit the ground flat."

"What about you?"

"I'll be fine. I'm immune to its poison, and Haggis tastes like dung to frogs."

"That won't stop it from crushing you to a pulp!"

"We don't have time to argue," McCools urged, as the frog lumbered closer. "Now run!"

They both started running along the path. The frog leaned all the way back on its hind legs then leapt up into the air.

"Dive!" McCools shouted.

Thumble Tumble threw herself onto the ground and the massive frog hopped right over the top of her, landing just behind McCools, who was still running along the path as fast as his three legs could carry him. The massive frog continued chasing him, and they both disappeared along the path.

Thumble Tumble scrambled to her feet and ran towards the pond. The water was indigo in colour, and in the centre there was a small object that seemed to be glowing.

'The key,' she thought, and pulled off her trainers with every intention of heading into the water. First, she dipped in her big toe and a cold chill ran down her spine. She jumped back, remembering the warning the Queen have given them. The words 'Nothing is what it seems' echoed in her head.

Kneeling at the water's edge, Thumble Tumble dipped her ring into the pond. A streak of rose-coloured light shot across surface of the water, revealing dozens of deadly spikes that rose up from the depths of the pond, waiting to impale any unsuspecting intruder.

The deadly spikes completely covered the pond, except for one row leading to the centre that had small flat platforms at the tip instead of spikes.

Thumble Tumble nervously placed her left foot onto the first platform. The platform was only two inches square, making it extremely difficult to balance. When she finally managed to steady herself on her tiptoes, she lifted her right foot. As soon as her foot left the ground she began to wobble. She looked down at the razor-sharp points surrounding her and promptly placed her foot back on the ground.

She took a deep breath. "You can do this!" she told herself. Very slowly, she lifted her right foot and placed it on the second platform and breathed a sigh of relief as she gradually made her way towards the middle of the pond, stepping lightly from platform to platform. But as she got closer to the centre, the platforms were getting further apart! She could no longer step between them and so started taking small jumps.

The last platform was a full metre away from the centre of Critter's Pond. Thumble Tumble looked all around but there was no other way to reach the glowing object. She bent down then leapt onto the platform landing with both feet, but it was too small, her left foot slipped and she lost her balance.

"Grab my feet," Smidge hollered from above her head. Thumble Tumble threw her hands up just managing to take hold of his right foot. The tiny bird soared into the sky. "Did you get the key?" he tweeted down towards her as she dangled, still clinging onto his foot.

"Not yet," she replied.

Smidge looked so furious, for a split second she thought he was going to drop her!

Just then the massive bat reappeared having finally caught up with its prey. It swooped towards them baring its bloodcurdling fangs.

"The key!" Smidge squawked, flying back towards the glowing object in the pond. "It's right there – grab it."

Thumble Tumble reached down, but the key was just out of reach.

The giant bat flew under them, then flicked backwards and aimed straight for Thumble Tumble.

"Let go!" Smidge screamed down at her. "I'll catch you, but you need to let go!"

Thumble Tumble released her grip and plunged towards the pond. The bat flew right over her head, but quickly swooped back around to get her.

Smidge flew down to catch her, but the bat swiped him with its wing, sending him spinning across the pond.

As Thumble Tumble plummeted down she reached forward and seized the glowing object just as she plunged into the water. There was an eruption of light from the centre of the pond. It shot straight up in the air, before spreading out across the whole island.

Thumble Tumble was still clinging onto the object she'd pulled from the pond as she sank under the water. To her surprise, she immediately popped back up to the surface and found herself sitting on a giant lily pad. The pond now looked very different from the one she'd fallen into. The water was clear blue with brightly coloured flowers scattered around the edges.

A little grey bat was fluttering above her head, looking very apologetic.

Thumble Tumble thought she must be dreaming. Smidge came hurtling down towards her, knocking the little bat into the pond as he charged past it.

"Did you get the key?" he tweeted.

"I got something," she replied, holding out the object she'd pulled from the pond. "But I'm not sure if it's what we're looking for!"

Chapter 17

Earie Lugger

Thumble Tumble and Smidge made their way back along the path to the entrance of the forest. It too had transformed. Splashes of golden sunshine shimmered through green bushes heavy with rosebuds.

Smidge was whizzing about above Thumble Tumble's head. "Just wait until I see those fairies," he chirped angrily. "We could've been killed – and all just to lift their stupid curse. They'd better have our key!"

"I'm sure they do," a familiar voice came echoing from up ahead.

As they drew closer, they could see McCools sitting at the side of the canyon with a small stick insect and a frog, playing a game of cards.

"This is Geoffrey," said McCools gesturing to the little red and yellow striped frog. "And you've both met Struan," he continued, pointing to the stick insect.

"They weren't quite themselves when Mogdred's curse was over them," he added, with a little chuckle.

"Glad you're finding this funny" Smidge snorted.

"And good luck getting across here without an oversized beastie to help you," he tweeted maliciously, as he flew across the gaping crevasse.

McCools didn't even look up, he simply continued his conversation with Thumble Tumble. "Struan is also known as the 'cloud keeper'," he told her.

Thumble Tumble looked at Struan curiously, wondering what a 'cloud keeper' did.

"I look after the clouds," he replied, as though she'd asked him the question she was thinking.

How on earth did he do that, she thought.

"I can hear your thoughts – it's an insect thing!" he explained, waving his two long antennae in the air.

"And yes, it is pretty cool," he nodded, responding to Thumble Tumble's next thought. "But it's not as cool as this," he said leaning over the edge of the canyon.

"Two travelling to the forest entrance" he called down.

As the stick insect stepped back from the edge, two small clouds drifted up out of the canyon and sat hovering at the edge.

"There you go," said Struan. "Two canyon clouds at your convenience."

Thumble Tumble wasn't sure what she was supposed to do. She'd never heard of a 'canyon cloud' before, let alone ridden on one!

McCools walked past her and hopped off the edge of the canyon onto one of the waiting clouds. He sat down and the cloud started drifting gently across to the opposite side.

Thumble Tumble stepped onto the remaining cloud. Her landing was a little less graceful, as she stumbled, causing her face to plonk onto the cloud, which promptly floated across the canyon.

"Thank you," she called back to Struan when she'd finally managed to sit up.

"Anything for Lizzie's daughter," the stick insect whispered under his breath.

Smidge was fluttering impatiently beside Sam when they arrived at the entrance to the forest.

"Where is the Queen?" asked McCools.

"She asked us to meet her at the castle," Sam replied, shrugging his shoulders.Night had fallen when they reached the castle. The moon was low in the sky with only a slither now covered by cloud. In the moonlight the castle's eight magnificent turrets sparkled orange and gold and the imposing iron gates had reverted into luscious hanging vines.

McCools frowned up at the moon. "Tomorrow it will be full," he whispered to Thumble Tumble.

"And we'll be safely home with the key," she replied chirpily, as they walked under the vines. But as soon as they set foot inside the castle an ear-piercing siren rang out. Intruder! Intruder! Intruder! went the alarm.

Within seconds they were surrounded by fairies, all brandishing small wands aimed directly at them.

"What's going on?" Smidge demanded, fluttering frantically in a circle.

"We have an intruder," said the Queen, emerging from the throng of fairies, Violet at her side.

"That's absurd!" Smidge blurted. "What are you trying to accuse us of?"

"Calm down, Tweetie-Pie," replied the Queen. "I'm not accusing you of anything."

"Good, then we'll take the key and be on our way!"

Smidge retorted, holding out his wing.

"Not so fast," the Queen replied slowly. "One of you is hiding something," she continued scanning them closely one by one. "Our defences always detect 'uninvited' guests."

Smidge flew behind Thumble Tumble's head. "This is ridiculous," he chirrupped. "You're just trying to keep the key!"

"It's you!" Violet hollered, pointing towards him.

She charged forward and flicked Thumble Tumble's ear lobe with her wand, to reveal a tiny person, hidden in the crevasse of her ear.

"It's an Earie Lugger," Violet announced, picking up the tiny creature.

The Earie Lugger was one centimetre tall and looked just like a minute person, except it had a long thin horn sticking out the side of its head in place of its left ear.

"What's an Earie Lugger?" Thumble Tumble gasped in horror at the thought of the creature living in her ear."A spy!" replied Violet, investigating the tiny creature more closely.

"This little character is working for a Witch," she continued, shaking the Earie Lugger in the air.

"Is it evil?" asked Thumble Tumble.

"Not necessarily," McCools piped up. "But the Witch who owns it, definitely is! Earie Luggers are very loyal creatures who are well looked after by their masters. It's only evil Witches who have them as good Witches don't believe in owning someone! They make very good spies as they hide just inside your ear, so they hear everything you hear. They then use that horn-like thing on their head to report the information back to their master, sending their

messages through the air waves so no one else can hear it."

"Do you think she's working for Mogdred?" asked Thumble Tumble.

"More than likely," he nodded.

Violet took a small silk pouch from her pocket and dropped the Earie Lugger inside. She then sprinkled a few drops of silver powder onto the pouch.

"It can't send out any more messages whilst it's in there," she said confidently.

"Okay, now that you've found your intruder, can you *please* give us our key?" Smidge squawked, his eyes bulging with impatience.

114

"I'm afraid I can't," replied the Queen, shaking her head. Smidge, Sam, McCools and Thumble Tumble all started at her in dismay.

"I can't give you the key, because Mogdred already has it!" the Queen continued.

"The Black Claw is the key. His hook transforms into the key that opens the chest."

"O.M.G." gasped Thumble Tumble. "Thank goodness Mogdred doesn't know, or all our friends would be dead by now!"

"We need to get back to Arran before she finds out," Sam said urgently.

"I'm afraid you're too late," came a loud cackle from behind them.

They turned around to see Smidge's body swell up like a balloon. The tiny bird had swollen to the size of a pig and he was still growing!

His wings began to stretch out at the sides of his body, then morphed into two arms, with hands which had long slender fingers.

His feet stretched down until they hit the floor, instantly transforming into legs. His eyes and beak disappeared into his swollen body that narrowed and stretched forming a torso from which a head popped out of the top. The head was facing away from them with long auburn hair that trailed onto the ground. The head then turned one hundred and eighty degrees revealing the beautiful features of Miss Malovent!

"I thought the castle didn't allow intruders?" Sam screeched to Violet and Ruby, who were also both looking on in astonishment at the shape-shifting Witch.

"I'm not an intruder, Sam," Miss Malovent said smarmily.

115

"I was invited in as a guest… remember?" she smiled.

"But now I feel I've outstayed my welcome, so I think I'll take my leave!" and a puff of orange smoke began to surround her.

Violet was still holding her wand. She aimed straight at Miss Malovent's heart.

"No!" screamed Thumble Tumble, pushing Violet's hand. The wand fired up into the castle ceiling as Miss Malovent disappeared into thin air.

Chapter 18

The Boat Book

Sam was still furious with Thumble Tumble as they made their way through the sulphur-infused air to get back to the ship.

"There's a shortcut to the shore," Violet said choking in the thick orange smoke. "Follow us."Violet and Queen Ruby took them down a spiral staircase to a wooden door. They rushed through the door and found themselves standing on the shore. Only moments had passed since Miss Malovent's disappearance, but there was no sign of her, or their ship!

"She's gone," Sam screamed at Thumble Tumble.

"I'm sorry, I just couldn't let Violet kill Smidge."

"She's NOT Smidge," he hollered back.

"There's no point in screaming at one another," McCools interjected. He turned to the Queen. "Can you get us back to Arran?" he asked pleadingly.

"I'm sorry… I can't," the Queen replied, shaking her head. "Although we can fly again, you're too heavy for us and we don't have a boat that we can enchant for you."

"Wait a minute," said McCools, frantically rummaging inside his scarf. He pulled out a small book with the picture of a boat on the cover. "*Ta da!*" he announced gleefully.

"I don't think your book about boats will help us," Thumble Tumble sighed. "Not unless it can show us how to build a boat in under a minute!"

"Oh, it can do way better than that," McCools smiled.

He opened the book at the centre pages and gently placed it cover up on the water. The book instantly started to grow! As it did so, the spine rose up, pulling the picture off the cover with it. The mast of a ship started to emerge from the spine. Once it had materialised at full size, two sails dropped down and then the book itself transformed into the hull of a ship.

Sam, Thumble Tumble and the two fairies stared on in astonishment.

"It's not a book *about* boats," grinned McCools. "It's a *boat book...* there's a huge difference!"

"Can you enchant this ship?" he nudged the Queen, who was still gaping at the sailing ship.

Queen Ruby gave herself a little shrug, snapping out of her trance. "Yes, I'm pretty sure I can!" she finally replied.

She nodded to Violet and the two of them flew up into the air. "It feels soooo good!" giggled Violet, as she twirled in the cool sea breeze.

"I know," Ruby smiled back. "But we've got plenty of time to fly later. Right now, we need to get that ship moving."

The Queen dived head-first into the sea.

"What's she doing," gasped Sam.

"You'll see," Violet replied, flying along the shoreline picking up long strands of seaweed.

After a few moments the Queen came shooting out of the water like a rocket, a surge of water at her feet acting like a propulsion engine. As she flew up into the air, two extraordinary creatures exploded through the water behind her. They looked like huge whales with hammer-heads for faces. Their navy-blue bodies were almost transparent against the water, unlike the ruby red circles around their eyes and the red horns piercing through their heads.

"What are they?" gulped Thumble Tumble.

"They're Devil Fish," Violet replied. She lay her collection of seaweed strands out on the shore.

Both Sam and Thumble Tumble gave her an uneasy look.

"Don't be put off by their name," she laughed. "They are very gentle creatures. The name is just because of their red horns."

Violet threw some powder over the seaweed strands before tossing them up into the air to Ruby.

Queen Ruby fluttered in front of the huge Devil Fish giving them instructions, but they were so far away, none of the others could hear what was being said.

When she had finished whispering to the fish, the Queen looped strands of seaweed around their horns, before firmly tying the other end of the seaweed strands to the prow of the ship.

After checking her knots were secure, she sprinkled some more powder onto the fixings. "That should do it," she announced.

Violet escorted Thumble Tumble, Sam and McCools to the gangplank attached to the ship and the three of them climbed on board. "The Devil Fish will get you home before sunset," The Queen told them. "I've given them secret directions to avoid the Crying Cliffs, so hopefully you'll beat Miss Malovent."

"Thank you so much," Thumble Tumble said.

The fairies turned to fly off, when Violet quickly swung back.

"What about this?" she asked, producing the small pouch with the Earie Lugger inside.

"I doubt it's loyal to Mogdred anymore," said McCools, shrugging his shoulders. "You may as well set it free."

"It can't stay here on Fairy Island," the Queen broke in.

"We'll take it with us then," Thumble Tumble said, holding out her hand.

Violet placed the tiny pouch onto Thumble Tumble's hand. It was barely the size of a sugar cube.

"I think you should keep it in the pouch until you're safely back on Arran," she cautioned. "You don't want Mogdred finding out you're on your way!"

Thumble Tumble nodded and carefully popped the tiny pouch into her dress pocket.

The Queen and Violet flew off the ship just as Sam stepped up to the helm. "Homeward bound," he shouted, as he didn't know the course they would be taking after the Queen had given her secret directions to the Devil Fish. The ship instantly soared through the water. It was travelling so fast that the two fairies had disappeared before Thumble Tumble got a chance to say goodbye.

It felt as though they were floating above the water as the giant fish hauled the ship on their mysterious journey home. It took exactly four hours from leaving Fairy Island to reach the shores of Arran.

The massive Devil Fish set the ship ashore on the beach

at the entrance to the Light and Dark Forest, then flicked the seaweed strands off their horns, before disappearing under the water.

"Jump!" hollered McCools, and he launched himself over the side of the ship onto the sand. Sam and Thumble Tumble followed suit without questioning his bizarre order.

As they landed on the hard-packed sand, they realised why McCools had got them to abandon ship so quickly. The ship was speedily transforming back into a book!

"I almost forgot it turns back into a book when you take it out of water," he gasped, picking up the little book and tucking it back into the fold in his scarf.

Chapter 19

Fairy Cake

Just as they were about to enter the Light and Dark Forest McCools put both arms out to stop them. "Before we go in here, we need to get you a wand," he said sternly.

"We've no time for that," replied Thumble Tumble, pushing his arm away. She marched into the forest, closely followed by Sam.

"It's too dangerous!" McCools insisted, jogging along the path beside them trying to keep up. "Besides, how can you help the others escape from Mogdred if you can't fight her?"

"We'll think of something," Thumble Tumble said, without slowing her pace. "We always do," she added with a cheeky little wink.

But McCools wasn't sure they would think of something. He had a very unsettling feeling in the pit of his stomach, and the fact it would soon be nightfall wasn't making him feel any better.

They followed the path through the forest until they reached the outskirts of the Tree Trolls' camp. They decided to cut through the trees from this point so as not to be detected by any of Mogdred's lookouts.

"Ouch, argh, ouch!" McCools groaned as they pushed through the thick foliage, with branches and twigs whacking him every few steps.

"Could you *be* any louder," Sam whispered sarcastically, as he moved agilely, avoiding the swinging branches. "We came this way to avoid being noticed. You may as well send up a flare with amount of noise you're making!"

"I'm sorry," winced McCools.

"Sorry?" a loud voice came echoing back at them.

The three of them stopped in their tracks just as another branch went smashing into McCools' stomach. Thumble Tumble swooped on him, placing her hand on his mouth to gag him.

"Why are you sorry?" the voice came booming again.

The three of them instantly recognised the voice... it belonged to Ugg!

Thumble Tumble and McCools peered through the foliage to see the greedy Tree Troll kneeling over a small glass cage. Skye was standing inside the cage, arms crossed, defiantly staring at her captor.

"I'm not sorry," she shouted up at him, stomping her foot.

"Then why did you say you were?" the Troll hollered into the cage, knocking Skye over with the force of his breath.

She jumped to her feet ready to retort when she caught a glimpse of Thumble Tumble through the bushes. She held her finger to her lips, willing Skye not to say anything.

"Okay, I am sorry," she conceded, looking up at Ogg wide-eyed.

"I'm sorry because I'm scared you are going to eat

me!" she pleaded.

"I'm sorry too," said Ugg, tilting his head. Skye took a step back, surprised by his comment.

"Sorry I can't eat you right now," he laughed loudly.

"I do love a 'good fairy'… cake!" He began laughing even louder, whacking his hand on his knee, impressed by his own wittiness. Huge droplets of saliva fell out of his open mouth and dropped through the cage onto Skye, covering her in a thick green mucous which made him laugh even more!

"What's so funny?" another familiar voice growled.

Ugg turned to his brother, grinning. "I told her I love a 'good fairy' cake," he chortled.

"Really?" Ogg replied in disdain, wiping the grin off Ugg's face.

"You better get her cleaned up before Mogdred arrives," he continued. "I've heard she likes her fairies hot, and we both know what good firewood you make!"

Ugg scowled at his twin, before stomping towards the centre of the camp to fetch some water.

Ogg leaned all the way down until his face was level with the cage. "You will be sorry," he whispered in an evil tone. "Only next time, it will be for real!"

Skye stood shivering as he got up and followed his brother into the campsite, smirking to himself.

As soon as the Trolls were out of sight, Thumble Tumble, McCools and Sam rushed over to the cage.

"Hold tight," said Thumble Tumble, as she yanked at the cage door, which didn't budge. "I can't get it open," she declared.

"Let me try," said Sam, but the door didn't budge for him either.

Skye sat down in the cage and began crying into her hands.

"We'll get you out of here," Thumble Tumble assured her, as all three of them linked arms around each other's waists and heaved, but the door barely wavered.

"We need the key," McCools conceded. "Or a wand," he said curtly, giving Thumble Tumble a hard stare.

"Perhaps we can pick the lock," she said desperately.

"With what?" he snapped.

Thumble Tumble paused for a moment then pulled the little pouch out of her pocket. "This!" she announced. She opened the pouch and tipped the Earie Lugger onto the palm of her hand.

"We have no interest in harming you," she addressed the Earie Lugger in a whisper.

The tiny creature didn't seem at all concerned by the situation. It stared back boldly at Thumble Tumble's giant face.

"Mogdred abandoned you," Thumble Tumble persisted. "So, you don't owe her anything!"

The Earie Lugger didn't respond at all. "We don't have time for all this small talk – if you'll pardon the pun," McCools let out a little giggle, for which he received a disapproving glare from Thumble Tumble.

"We'll let you go, but first you need to do something for us," he said.

The Earie Lugger raised its left eyebrow.

"We need you to pick that lock." McCools pointed to the cage where Skye sat crying inside.

"Can you do it?"

The Earie Lugger examined the lock, then nodded.

Thumble Tumble placed her hand in front of the cage door. The Earie Lugger stepped off the tip of her middle finger and disappeared inside the lock.

There were a few clicking sounds followed by a raucous screech that made everyone's jaws clench. The tooth-grinding noise lasted for a few seconds before the cage door swung open. Skye flew out of the cage, shaking off the green mucous.

"Where's the Earie Lugger?" Sam enquired as he peered into the empty lock.

"She's gone!" McCools replied anxiously. "And I suggest we follow suit before those Trolls get back."

All four of them quickly headed back towards the foliage when they heard a swooshing sound above them, followed by an unforgettable squawk!

Chapter 20

The Guardian

Miss Malovent was once again masquerading as Smidge. She immobilised them with a single flap of her wing, casting a freezing spell over all four of them.

She then summoned Ugg and Ogg to carry their statue-like bodies into the campsite where the Goblin Pirates were held prisoner. The Trolls dropped their captives onto the floor of the makeshift prison, incarcerating the other Goblins. Their rigid bodies reverberated off the hard ground.

"What have you done to them?" demanded Jake, squirming to try to free his hands from behind his back.

Ugg and Ogg just stood behind the wall that held them prisoner and laughed.

"You'll pay for this!" Jake yelled.

"You're probably right," Ogg said nastily. "I often suffer from indigestion after eating Goblin Stew!" and he howled with laughter.

"Enough taunting," ordered Miss Malovent, who had reverted into human form.

128

"There will be plenty of that when Mogdred returns." She pointed her wand at Thumble Tumble and mumbled a few words. Within seconds, Thumble Tumble was able to move again, but before she could even stand up her hands were bound with a pair of handcuffs behind her back.

"That's better!" mused Miss Malovent. She carried out the same exercise on the others before transforming back into Smidge and flying off in the direction of the shore.

"Are you guys all right?" gasped Thumble Tumble, as she glanced along the line of weary looking Goblins.

Tibbs was definitely the worse for wear, his toes still seeping blood through his stained bandages. Beside him, Flynn resembled a skeleton loosely wrapped in skin, he was so thin! Will, Jake and Toby had been tied back to back with a thick bristly rope. The captain was lying on the floor at the end of the row. He had been gagged as well as having his hands and feet bound together.

"We need to get out of here," urged McCools. "Mogdred knows about the key," he nodded towards the captain.

The captain started writhing on the ground, desperately trying to loosen the gag so he could speak.

"Save your energy," McCools told him. "You'll need it when Mogdred arrives."

Night had already fallen and the full moon shone down, casting shadows onto the wall that penned them in.

Skye gave McCools a grave look. She hoped he too realised how vulnerable Thumble Tumble was, now that the protective power of her fairy dust had worn off.

"If only I could reach into my pocket," she said in anguish, as she struggled to free her tiny hands from the magical handcuffs Miss Malovent had used. But the more she struggled the tighter the handcuffs became.

"We've all tried to get them off," sighed Tibbs. "But the harder we try the tighter they become." He spun round on his bottom to show them his hands, which were now so tightly bound by the handcuffs they had turned black from lack of circulation.

"What about you guys?" Thumble Tumble looked anxiously towards Jake, Toby and Will.

"Same thing," replied Jake. "If any of us move, the ropes tighten – we can hardly breath they're so tight!"

"Breathing... it's so overrated!" came a vile chuckle from outside the prison wall, closely followed by the familiar stench of Mogdred.

As she stepped out of the shadows into the moonlight, her features sharpened. The dark hollows where her cheeks had once been had sunk so deep into her face, they made her eyes protrude, as though two golf balls had been stuck into her eye sockets.

"A little birdy told me I sent you on a bit of a wild goose chase," she whispered eerily. As she spoke, she created a trail of icy condensation in the air.

"No matter... because now I have The Witches' Eye and the key to Medusa's chest." She flicked her finger and the trail of icy air started spiralling towards Thumble Tumble. It wound around her neck momentarily before drifting down to the handcuffs binding her hands, which fell to the ground.

Mogdred spread her long fingers towards Thumble Tumble to collect The Eye.

"It's not mine to give," Thumble Tumble snapped. "I promised I'd return it, and unless it's given willingly, it won't work – you know that!"

"Would you rather hold onto that Eye and watch your friends die?" seethed Mogdred.

"You're going to kill them anyway," Thumble Tumble said defiantly.

"Yes, that is true," nodded Mogdred. "But if you give me The Eye I promise it will be a quick, painless death for them."

"I don't think there is a less painless way to be cooked alive by Trolls," Thumble Tumble retorted.

The Tree Trolls grinned at one another, salivating at the thought.

"What if I agree to evaporate them completely without them being eaten?" quizzed Mogdred. She was now standing within the prison walls, her gaze burning into Thumble Tumble as she waited for a reply.

Ugg and Ogg suddenly stopped grinning. "That wasn't the deal!" Ugg hollered at the top of his lungs, unable to hide his rage. And for once, Ogg was in agreement with his brother. They both stomped angrily towards the prison.

"I've told you two before – deals are made to be broken!" boomed Mogdred. She rose into the air then blasted the Trolls with a spell that catapulted them miles away.

"Now, where was I?" she resumed as she floated back towards the ground. She glanced along the row of Goblins. As her gaze fell upon Jake, she remembered how upset Sam had become when she'd chosen him before.

"You" she snapped, waiving her finger at Jake. The ropes around Jakes body untwined and he floated to his feet in front of her.

She placed her nail under his chin and tilted his head up slightly, piercing the skin. A single drop of blood slid

131

down his neck.

"Leave him alone!" Sam begged. He shot Thumble Tumble a glance of desperation.

"Well?" spat Mogdred.

Thumble Tumble slowly reached down into her pocket, but quickly pulled her hand out again.

"No! I won't do it!" she insisted. "I made a promise."

Mogdred slapped Jake to the ground, grabbing Thumble Tumble by the throat in his place. She grinned up at the full moon as she lifted Thumble Tumble clean off the ground. "I'd like to see you keep that promise when you're dead!" she hissed.

There was a sudden swoosh in the air and Smidge came flying into the campsite. "Perhaps we should wait to see if we can open the chest before we kill her?" he tweeted. "We wouldn't want to kill her and then find out we still need her – would we?"

Mogdred reluctantly released her grip. "I will deal with you later," she growled.

Smidge transformed back into Miss Malovent. Standing beside Mogdred, Miss Malovent's beauty emphasised how grotesquely ugly Mogdred had become.

"I don't like you in this form," Mogdred said jealousy. "Why don't you transform into a toad or a snake?"

Miss Malovent didn't respond. Instead, she grabbed the captain by his feet and threw him over the prison wall.

Mogdred drifted straight through the wall after him and Miss Malovent turned to follow suit. Just as she did, she mouthed down to Thumble Tumble "Now we're even!"

Thumble Tumble sat up on the ground examining her finger. The reason she'd pulled her hand out of her pocket was because something inside her pocket had jagged into

132

her index finger. Right on the very tip of her finger were ten tiny pin pricks in the shape of a bite mark!

Thumble Tumble gently felt back inside her pocket and to her utter surprise was greeted by the Earie Lugger who'd fled earlier.

"What are you doing in there?" she whispered. "If Mogdred finds you, she'll kill you for betraying her!"

"I didn't betray Mogdred," the tiny creature replied without moving its lips.

"Wow, you're telepathic," said Thumble Tumble.

"Not quite. I use magical radio waves to communicate with the aid of my horn," the creature pointed to the horn sticking out of the side of its head.

"There are different radio waves for Witches, Trolls, Haggis, etc! So only you can hear me just now."

Thumble Tumble looked over at the others who were all staring back at her very strangely.

"They think you're talking to yourself!" the Earie Lugger laughed.

"But you've still not told me why you're here," said Thumble Tumble.

The little creature adjusted its horn. "I'm here to save you." Everyone gasped. For some reason, they could all now hear the creature speak.

"I am the Guardian of The Eye. My mission is to help you return it to its rightful owners."

"So, you're not Mogdred's spy?" gasped Sam.

"Not me!" The Earie Lugger shook its head. "I belong to the hags of the cave."

"Why do *they* want you to save Thumble Tumble?" quizzed McCools warily.

"They want their Eye back. They know your intention

is to return The Eye and so they have instructed me to help you escape so that you will give it to me of your own free will. Set me down beside the fairy," the Earie Lugger instructed.

The tiny creature hopped into the lock on Skye's handcuffs, which opened in a flash.

"Quickly, sprinkle the Witch with your fairy dust," it said, before crawling into the lock securing McCools' handcuffs.

The Earie Lugger spent the next few minutes releasing all six Goblin pirates from their shackles.

"Now all we need to do is get through the wall," it smiled

The Goblin pirates dropped their heads in dismay. They'd all been inside Witches' prisons before and knew the walls were protected by very powerful magic.

Tibbs picked up a twig and threw it at the wall. As soon as the twig touched the wall it disintegrated. He then threw another over the top. Again, the second it passed over the wall it turned to dust.

"Why didn't the captain frazzle when Miss Malovent threw him over?" asked Thumble Tumble.

"She cast a spell just as she threw him," Tibbs replied gloomily.

"Honestly!" piped up the Earie Lugger, frowning at the defeated looking crew. "I thought you lot were pirates? You have one of the most precious magical treasures right here, and you don't even know it!"

They all stared at the Earie Lugger blankly.

"*The Protector*!" it announced, sounding exasperated.

"I'm afraid I am pretty useless," Thumble Tumble replied despondently. "I lost my wand."

"You don't need a wand," the Earie Lugger said, scrutinising Thumble Tumble's pinkie ring. "The magic lives within you. All you need is *that* ring to help you channel it!"

Chapter 21

Bird Cage

Thumble Tumble stood in front of the wall. She placed her hands out in front of her and focused all her energy down through her fingertips. There was a tingling feeling then a blast of rose-coloured light shot out from her fingertips and blasted off the wall.

The blast created a puff of smoke that drifted upwards, gradually disappearing into the atmosphere. Unfortunately, the wall did not disappear with it!

"Do you think it worked?" Thumble Tumble asked the others.

Tibbs picked up a twig and threw it towards the wall. It evaporated just like the two before it had.

"I'm afraid not," he said and shook his head.

"You need to focus more." the Earie Lugger pressed. "Stop thinking about the ring, it's only an amulet. Think about saving your friends and the magic will come."

'I hope you're right,' Thumble Tumble thought to herself, stretching her arms back out. She closed her eyes and started to think about all the adventures she'd

had with Skye and McCools. A warm tingling feeling flowed through her entire body as she remembered their many escapades together. Next thing she knew, she shot backwards, landing on her bottom with the force of the blast that had launched out of her hands.

When she opened her eyes, she was filled with disappointment to see the wall still standing between them and their freedom.

She glanced over to McCools apologetically, only to see him grinning back at her.

"Why so happy?" she asked glumly.

"Turn around," he said, swirling his stubby finger.

Thumble Tumble looked over her shoulder, then gasped with joy when she found herself standing on the other side of the wall. She had somehow managed to transport all of them out of the prison!

She quickly clamped her hands over her mouth, remembering Mogdred was not far away.

"My mission is complete," the tiny Earie Lugger announced abruptly, standing on the tip of Thumble Tumble's nose.

"It certainly is," replied Thumble Tumble digging deep into her pocket. "I believe this belongs to you," she said, holding The Eye out in the palm of her hand.

The Earie Lugger jumped off her nose landing on her palm beside The Eye. "You are a Witch of your Word!" It announced, before placing its horn against The Eye. And then they both disappeared in a cloud of dust.

Just before evaporating, the Earie Lugger dropped something into Thumble Tumble's pocket.

"What's that?" asked McCools.

Thumble Tumble brought the item out of her pocket.

"It's a trap," she announced in a whisper, holding up the glass cage the Trolls had used to capture Skye.

"If we can get Miss Malovent to transform, we can capture her in here. Then we only have Mogdred to deal with."

"Only," gulped McCools.

"Leave it to me," piped up Skye, and she flew off in the direction of Mogdred and Miss Malovent.

They were standing beside the chest with the captain hovering above it in mid-air as the pair of them took it in turn to torture him.

"Leave him alone, you, ugly old hag," Skye called out as she flew over their heads.

Mogdred fired a bolt that singed Skye's hair as it skimmed past her.

"Not you!" Skye shouted down. "Her," she chortled pointing at Miss Malovent.

Mogdred couldn't hide her satisfaction at Miss Malovent being called a hag.

Furious, Miss Malovent transformed into Smidge and shot after Skye. He had his razor-sharp claws poised to rip the delicate water fairy to pieces.

Skye dived towards the wall surrounding the prison, with Smidge in close pursuit. But as Smidge flew towards the prison, he could see it was empty. Sensing something was wrong he quickly changed direction. "I'm not that stupid," he chirped over his shoulder, and he flew straight into a huge net being held up by Tibbs and Sam.

"Quick, put him in the cage," hollered Sam. "Before he transforms." Tibbs tipped the tiny bird into the glass cage and locked the door just as Smidge uttered the last words of the transforming spell.

"Too late," sniggered Tibbs. "I'm afraid your magic doesn't work inside the cage!" he said, placing the glass cage beside the prison wall.

Mogdred hadn't noticed that Smidge had disappeared. She was too busy trying to force the captain to open the chest.

"Open it, or I'll pull your arm from your body and open it myself," she shrieked, tugging his arm.

The captain tried to mumble something through his gag as he nodded down towards the chest.

Mogdred flicked a finger, removing the gag.

"I've never really liked this claw," he smiled cheekily. "So, if it's all the same to you, I'll not open the chest and you can have the arm!"

Mogdred hit him in the stomach with a bolt so strong he flew ten feet in the air before landing in front of the chest.

Dazed, he opened his eyes to a blurred vision floating towards him. Unfortunately, his sight quickly returned, revealing Mogdred's hideous face only a few inches away from his own.

"Okay, I'll open it," he panted. "On one condition."

Mogdred frowned intensely as she pressed her nose against his head. "What Condition?" she seethed.

"That you have a breath mint," he burst out laughing.

Enraged, Mogdred took a step back. "I may not have the pleasure of opening the chest, but I will have the pleasure of watching you die instead." She raised her hand ready to perform a death curse.

"I wouldn't do that," came a voice from behind her.

Thumble Tumble was standing over the wide-open chest holding a long purple wand aimed straight at

Mogdred's head.

Mogdred paused, staring in disbelief at the scene unravelling in front of her eyes.

Thumble Tumble was gripping the wand in both hands, shaking from head to toe as she focussed all her energy into the wand.

Mogdred knew she wouldn't be able to kill the captain before Thumble Tumble set off her blast.

"No!" she shrieked in horror. She fired a bolt just missing Thumble Tumble then snapped her fingers and disappeared in a cloud of grey ash along with Smidge and the cage.

Chapter 22

Batons to the Ready

"How on earth did you manage to open my chest?" coughed Captain Black Claw, when he'd managed to pick himself up off the ground.

"I don't know," replied Thumble Tumble, still shaking as she stood there, with the wand wavering in his direction.

"Well, the evil Witches have gone now, so perhaps it would be a good time to lower that conductor's baton?" the captain indicated.

She looked confused.

"You do know that stick isn't a wand – don't you?" he said jovially.

Thumble Tumble shook her head.

"It's a baton that belonged to a very famous conductor: Bat Hoven, the great vampire conductor! Thankfully it would appear that Mogdred doesn't know the difference between a wand and a baton either." he laughed.

"I'll need to take it back," he said, carefully removing the baton from Thumble Tumble's clenched hand. "But for your bravery, you can choose something else from the

141

chest as a reward."

"Won't Medusa get angry if I take one of her treasures?
Thumble Tumble asked warily.

"I'm pretty sure she would if this was her chest," he
replied. "But it's not Medusa's. It's my treasure chest. I
put the head of Medusa on the lid as a deterrent to scare
people off from trying to steal it... clearly that didn't work
out too well!" he chortled.

"You mean to tell me we went through all of that, and
the chest doesn't even possess dark magic?" McCools
reeled at the thought.

"I wouldn't quite say that," the captain replied.
"Although the chest doesn't belong to Medusa, it does
contain a lot of dangerous treasures, that in Mogdred's
hands would be fatal!"

He picked a small green ball out of the chest with his
claw hand. "This, for example!"

"What is it?" asked Thumble Tumble, screwing up her
nose.

"It's a Gigantaball," the captain exclaimed. "If you rub
it three times it turns into a ravenous giant, who's at your
command."

"Wow, Mogdred would love that!" said Thumble
Tumble taking a step back.

"Anyway" he continued, placing the ball back into its
holder inside the chest. "What would you like as a gift to
thank you for saving us?"

Thumble Tumble leaned over the chest. Her eyes
widened as she surveyed the multitude of treasures packed
inside. There were dozens of necklaces and bracelets all
embossed with precious gems along with an array of
different shaped trinket boxes and jewels.

142

Right at the bottom of the chest there was a tiny silver object. Thumble Tumble picked it up. "I'd like this" she said. "Although I don't actually know what it is," she added, twisting it between her fingers.

"It's a thimble," smiled McCools. "People wear them on their finger when they're sewing to stop the needle from pricking them."

"Oh!" she replied, now looking a little disappointed by her selection.

"Not this thimble," the Black Claw announced excitedly. "Pop it on."

Thumble Tumble placed the thimble onto her finger and immediately disappeared.

"It's an invisibility thimble," gasped McCools.

"Not quite," the captain answered. "Be careful," he said, grabbing McCools by the arm. "Look down."

There on the ground stood a tiny two-centimetre tall Thumble Tumble.

"Now take it off," he said.

The instant she took off the thimble, Thumble Tumble sprouted back to her original size.

"It's a shrinking thimble," he proclaimed.

Thumble Tumble was now beaming so widely that her jaws were hurting.

She still had the small pouch the fairies had given her to transport the Earie Lugger, so she carefully placed the thimble in it and popped it back into her pocket.

The captain then addressed his crew. "Get to your feet, you scurvy dogs," he hollered with a crooked smile on his face.

"Aye, aye," the crew replied in unison, as they stood to attention, each of them grinning from ear to ear, delighted to be back under the command of their captain.

"We're going to be stuck on this slimy piece of land until we can rebuild our ship," he continued bellowing at the top of his lungs.

"You might be able to leave sooner than you think," said McCools, producing a small book from the fold in his scarf.

"A book about boats," frowned the captain. "Thanks for your help McCools, but we're pirates – we know how to build a ship!"

"It's no ordinary book, captain," Sam interrupted, winking across to McCools. "Trust me!"

The Goblin pirates picked up their treasure chest and followed McCools to the beach where he placed the book into the water.

McCools, Sam and Thumble Tumble watched the look of amazement on the crew's faces as the huge sailing ship rose out of its pages.

There were a few red eyes as Sam said his goodbyes to Thumble Tumble and McCools, before the Goblin pirates set sail on their next adventure.

Waving them off, Thumble Tumble wondered what her next adventure might be, not realising it was lurking on the sand only a few feet away from her!

www.thumbletumble.co.uk
Find out more about this series, latest news, events and
when the next book will be available.

All books in the series can be ordered from the Thumble
Tumble website and are also available from your local
bookshop and online retailers.
www.scottishbookstore.com

Or by post from:
Thumble Tumble, PO Box 27132 Glasgow G3 9ER
Email:info@thumbletumble.co.uk

Follow the Adventure!

Don't miss books 1–3 of the Thumble Tumble series, *Thumble Tumble and the Ollpheist*, *Thumble Tumble and the Cauldron of Undry* and *Thumble Tumble and the Eagalach Cup*.

THUMBLE TUMBLE
AND THE OLLPHEIST

A. H. PROCTOR

Thumble Tumble
and the
Cauldron of Undry

A.H. Proctor

THUMBLE TUMBLE
and the
Eagalach Cup

A.H. Proctor

About the Author

A.H. Proctor is a successful businesswoman, wife and mother who has unashamedly lived in a fantasy world for most of her life. Captivated from childhood by fairy stories and the world of the Brothers Grimm, her fertile imagination was held in check until she took her own young children to the beautiful and mystical Isle of Arran. When, one day, they asked her to tell them a story of Witches and dragons, the floodgates opened. Inevitably, Angela could not resist taking it a stage further and she began to write, and so the Thumble Tumble books set on mysterious Arran were born.

First Published in the UK in 2019 by
FORTH BOOKS
www.forthbooks.co.uk

Text copyright ©2019 A.H. Proctor
Cover and illustrations G. Howells

ISBN 978-1-909266-17-9 Thumble Tumble and the Goblin Pirates – bk 4
ISBN 978-1-909266-18-6 Thumble Tumble and the Goblin Pirates – bk 4 (e-book)

A CIP record of this book is available
from the British Library.

Typeset by Main Point Books, Edinburgh.
Printed and bound in the UK.

and the

Goblin Pirates

A.H. PROCTOR

FORTH BOOKS